# SOUTHERN GOTHIC

## Other Books by Dale Wiley

*The Intern*
*Sabotage*
*Kissing Persuasive Lips*

## Coming Soon

*The Jefferson Bible*

# SOUTHERN GOTHIC

A NOVEL

DALE WILEY

Southern Gothic



Author Photo Credit: Robyn Lyn Anderson
www.robynlynphotography.com



ISBN: 978-1-944109-06-6

Published by Vesuvian Books
www.vesuvianbooks.com

Printed in the United States of America

10 9 8 7 6 5 4 3 2 1

*To Mary, Sara and Matt, who continue to surprise and amaze.*

*To Jennifer and Terrie, for their love of books and all the memories and inspiration.*

# TABLE OF CONTENTS

# PART I
# HEAVEN

"To put meaning in one's life may end in madness,
But life without meaning is the torture
Of restlessness and vague desire—
It is a boat longing for the sea and yet afraid."

—Edgar Lee Masters, *Spoon River Anthology*

# CHAPTER 1

The letter came to the bookstore Wednesday morning, postmarked Savannah. The stationery was expensive and regal, and although it was not embossed with any initials, it felt important. It was addressed to *Ms. Meredith Harper, Southern Gothic Bookstore* in a powerful script, the angular letters formed with a fountain pen. The thick strokes of blue ink looked familiar to the recipient; she knew the handwriting but couldn't place it.

The envelope's inner lining was the same dark blue as the ink. She lifted the note card out gingerly, not wanting to smear any message:

> *Dear M:*
> *I will call you today. An opportunity awaits.*
> *Yours forever,*
> *M*

She thought about showing it to her assistant, Nate, but something stopped her. She liked the mystery. She probably should be a little more alarmed by such a personal letter, but she couldn't help being thrilled at the thought of a secret admirer—and one who wrote her a letter. It felt like an entry into another world, one not marred by insistent emails and the soul-killing *ping* of never-ending text messages. On a day when she had much to do, it lifted her spirits and gave her a little secret to carry in her pocket.

Months before a space on Broughton Street had opened up near the City Market, where the smells of good pizza and the light, drunk laughs of passersby made every trip seem an adventure. It guaranteed year-round foot traffic and plenty of late-night visitors on the nights she kept the place open later than normal. The bookstore was Meredith's gift to herself, a reimagining of her life and priorities after she divorced Lance, her one-note song of disappointment. She asked for the divorce, afraid she might join him in the river of constant, mild annoyance, which had pulled him under. She needed to pull back the drapes and let some light into her house to remember what inspired her in the first place.

She wanted to write, to tell the world the story of *Red Ribbon*, a tale that had haunted her for years. She had painstakingly written and revised until the manuscript sparkled—good enough to make it on the shelves of her bookstore—but nothing ever materialized. She wanted to be in the company of Flannery and Eudora and other writers she adored, but she would have to settle for being a purveyor of their work.

Although Lance had lost his drive, his wit, and his waistline, he never lost the ability to sit heavy on her dreams. One evening, while she struggled to find the right character motivation, Lance had come home drunk and told her to quit wasting her time—she'd never be more than a fan girl, a writer wannabe chasing a dream she'd never catch. It still felt like a clammy hand on her shoulder.

Over the last year, she almost quit caring what Lance thought, but he still knew how to stick a landing in her brain. He constantly told her she was too pretty to be a writer. He didn't mean it as a compliment. Just another example of a person being completely out of touch with how his words felt to anyone else but himself.

Lance was right about the pretty. Meredith was tiny, barely reaching five feet, with deep blue eyes. She kept her brown hair long, unlike many of her friends who reached forty and immediately chopped it all off. Since she opened up the store, she heard every variation of *sexy librarian*, but in her case, it made some sense. Although she didn't flaunt it, she had been blessed with curves and could rock a little black dress when she needed to. She didn't dress up much, preferring jeans and a button-up to the more formal get-ups sported in Savannah, but her bright personality made everything she did seem effortless.

The men who frequented the shop doted on her, testing to see if she was ready to start dating again; she was—but not with them. Yet it comforted her to know they admired her for her brains and book choices as well as the way she looked in a cocktail dress. Chalk one up for sexy librarians.

At least the bookstore gave her the feeling of being in demand, involved in something important and worthwhile. And now she had a mysterious admirer. Hopefully a new opportunity to lose herself in the right kind of romance.

Her shop also had a kitchen to bake in—her nonliterary passion—so people came by to eat and browse the shelves. The bookstore smelled heavenly, a wonderful combination of cinnamon and books—dusty literary relics and fresh new novels straight from the publishers. She christened the place *Southern Gothic*, and a star was born.

Meredith graced the cover of many regional magazines, left hand on her hip, her story on everyone's lips. She added a small musical collection up front, featuring Lucinda Williams and John Prine and the queen of strange Southern songs, Tanya Tucker. The establishment struck the perfect mood for downtown Savannah, half hip and unusual, half buttoned-up and on point. Thanks to the bookstore, Meredith presided over all of it, the new dame of downtown.

Meredith fiddled with the display. She absent-mindedly rearranged a Harlan Coben endcap, interacted with guests, and made decisions with

Nate about the next day's reading. But mostly, she thought about the letter. She picked up the envelope and opened it again. Who was *M*?

The call finally came in the afternoon.

From the back of the store, she heard Nate answer the phone and mumble something before walking toward the bakery.

"It's for you." He handed her the cordless phone.

She sighed and put it to her ear. "This is Meredith."

A man's voice hissed at her, a combination of contempt and what might be amusement. "You need to come home."

"Excuse me? Who is this?"

"Come home," the voice hissed again.

Then the line went dead.

Meredith, rattled, handed the phone back to Nate, who looked at her expectantly.

"Wrong number, I guess." She shrugged her shoulders and went back to her inventory.

Several minutes later, Nate returned with the phone in his hand.

"It's for you again," he said apologetically.

She stared at it for a moment before putting it to her ear.

"Come—"

"Who is this?" Meredith yelled.

The line went dead, again.

Nate looked at her in alarm. "Is everything okay?"

Meredith shook her head. "Just another creeper." She handed him the phone and went back to working on the end cap.

Nate reappeared sometime later with an unnerved look on his face. Meredith's heart raced and she quickly glanced to see if he was bringing her the phone again, but his hands were empty.

"What's wrong?" she asked.

"I need you to come look at something. Just to make sure I'm not reading it wrong."

Meredith nodded, mildly annoyed and a little uneasy. A prank call would never rattle Nate. She followed him over to the main checkout area, confused. Nate still wouldn't look her in the eye.

"What is all this cloak and dagger routine?"

Nate finally looked at her. "Before you pick up and talk to him, please look at the caller ID and tell me what you see."

Meredith's heart plummeted. What did he mean?

Then she saw it.

The phone displayed 912-555-7769. She looked at it and blinked, then read the row beneath it. HARPER, MER. It was her landline.

The call was coming from inside her house.

# CHAPTER 2

Blood pounded in her ears. What the hell was going on? Meredith picked up the phone, but the line was dead. She looked at Nate. He met her gaze this time. She tried to look calm for him, but panic welled up inside her.

She grabbed her cell to dial 9-1-1 but then thought better of it. There had to be some reasonable explanation like neighborhood kids. Except she had received the note followed by these suspicious phone calls. She didn't want to go home without some kind of back up.

Meredith turned toward Nate, knowing he had a crush on her. "Want to help me solve a mystery?"

Nate looked surprised. "Aren't the police more suited for that?"

She suppressed an eye roll. "I agree, but there's no use wasting valuable taxpayer dollars on a prank call. I just want to know what's going on. It's probably nothing." She grabbed her keys from the counter and headed for the door.

"Wait." Nate ran to catch up.

Nate was a catch for her professionally. He had attended Emory, studied literature, and was in the middle of a first novel she had asked to read, but he had yet to give her. He was thin and dressed very well—lots of sweaters and scarves. He wore glasses that begged to be taken off his face for a kiss. If he were fifteen years older, she would sweep him up. But she didn't want to babysit. She needed a man.

And the crush. She knew it would come someday—the awkward moment when she would have to parry his thrust. Oh, she didn't want to do that. This boy was nice and sweet and everything you'd train your son to be. He was probably more mature and interesting than her ex-husband, but she wanted more. She loved her life and her surroundings enough now—yes, she wanted companionship again, and yes, she would love a little romance. But she wasn't going to take herself out of her comfort zone unless it felt right.

Outside, it was cool and breezy; fall waited just around the corner. Clouds blocked half the sun, weakening the heat that typically beat down on the coast.

The quick drive to her house seemed to take forever.

"What are we doing?" Nate asked.

Meredith laughed. "I don't think there'll be a serial killer involved if that's what you're thinking."

He toyed with his glasses. "What do you know that you're not telling me?"

She didn't know why she wouldn't tell him about the letter, but she didn't. Before she had to make up an answer, they had arrived.

She parked across the street from her house and looked around. Her neighbor Mrs. Coleman sat on her porch sipping iced tea.

Meredith went in the back way and past the carriage house like she always did. She used the carriage house as a garage. Years of prior residents' projects, including a couple of old cabinets and an army trunk, too heavy to move, filled every nook. She looked for the Louisville Slugger, a Dale Murphy model, Lance kept in the corner. It wasn't there. Had Lance finally picked it up?

She expanded her search, but it still eluded her. Was Lance behind all of this? She shook her head. No, it was way too colorful for him.

Meredith ignored Nate's look of a thousand questions and headed around the back side of the house and on to the porch. She slowed her breathing, hoping to hear anything.

"Do you smell a cigar?" Nate asked, commenting on the strange whiff in the air.

She shook her head. "Cloves."

"We should call the police," Nate said, eyeing his way back to the car.

She turned to face him "Oh, come on, we've got this." She felt sheepish saying that while sweat poured from her armpits. She hoped Nate didn't notice how close she was to retreating too.

"Anyone here?" she said forcefully. The kitchen appeared just as she left it, dirty dishes piled in the sink. She couldn't help but feel momentarily embarrassed about Nate seeing the mess. She tiptoed through the hall to the living room. Nothing looked out of place there either. Now the upstairs.

Halfway up, the closed bedroom door worried her, but she couldn't remember whether she had closed it or not. At the top of the stairs, she grabbed a pair of old brass candlesticks from one of the bookshelves, like something out of *Clue*, and handed one to Nate. Then she flung open the bedroom door.

Nothing.

They peered in the closet, under the bed, and behind the doors. Then they combed through each upstairs room, finding nothing and looking at each other uneasily. She still held her breath, nerves getting the best of her.

Then Meredith burst out laughing. "I think we can talk now."

Nate sighed and laughed too. "I'm not cut out for this cloak and dagger stuff."

"Well, I can at least pay you in chess pie." She smiled as Nate's eyes caught fire.

"Love it. No extra withholdings."

She gave them each big slices, and they sat down, eating the first few bites in silence.

"Thanks for coming. I know looking for serial killers isn't really in your job description."

"Happy to. I always love a good damsel rescue."

She smiled. "Thanks, Nate."

He furrowed his brow. "Are you sure you're okay?"

"It's probably neighborhood kids like I said."

He shook his head. "I don't know, Meredith. Let me look in the living room again. Maybe we missed something the first time."

She couldn't be mad at him for being protective. "Ok. Thanks, Nate." She watched him leave and turned to scan the room one last time as well—and stopped dead in her tracks.

Inside on her kitchen doorknob, someone had tied a garish red ribbon.

# CHAPTER 3

The red ribbon, made of silk and tied neatly in a bow, rested on her door, mocking her, a reminder of her biggest failure. Without thinking, she raced over to it and undid the bow before Nate saw it. She stuffed it in her back pocket, feeling oddly embarrassed.

No one else had seen the greatness in her book. Her friends were encouraging, but no one remembered it now. She thought it had the right combination of ancient ghosts and modern troubles that would be appeal to readers, but she couldn't find the right advocate, someone who shared her passion for the book and would actually do something about it.

She understood how rare it was to get published. So many people had dreams of being writers, but few actually succeeded. With *Red Ribbon*, she had never wanted anything so bad and had failed so miserably.

"Hey, Nate, I've got this," she called out to the living room. "You mind walking back to the store?" She hoped she sounded confident.

Nate came back around the corner, looking skeptical. "Of course. But are you sure?"

"Absolutely. I'll try and stop by later."

When Nate disappeared around the corner, she sat down on the porch swing, woozy from the adrenaline still coursing through her body. She pulled the ribbon out of her pocket and rubbed her thumb across the smooth satin finish. A red ribbon. Only someone who knew her very well could hurt her so perfectly. She lived two years with her book baby, the one she knew without a doubt would make her a fortune. But it arrived stillborn, never to breathe this world's air.

Lance seemed like a prime suspect, but he didn't smoke clove cigarettes, and he certainly wasn't deep or creative enough for this kind of gameplay. She had sent the manuscript to so many people; but who was mean enough to tease her about her failures like this?

"Meredith. How are you, darling?"

Meredith snapped her head up. "Hi, Mrs. Coleman." How long had she been staring at the ribbon? She quickly put it back in her pocket and pasted a smile on her face.

Mrs. Coleman shuffled up the walk, garden shears tucked in the pocket of her smock, wearing her ancient floppy-brimmed hat with the chinstrap cinched tight, and carrying a tray with two glasses of iced tea.

*The sweet thing … she shouldn't have.* Originally from Sea Island—Georgia's wealthiest neighborhood—Mrs. Coleman had lived in Savannah for over twenty years and took her neighborly duties seriously. Meredith sprang to her feet and ran down the steps. Out of all her neighbors, Meredith liked Mrs. Coleman the most. She doted on the old lady, who, like an eccentric spinster aunt, was a little wacky but still charming. "Let me take the tray."

"It's so unusual to see you home during the day. I thought you might need a little refreshment."

An inveterate gardener, Mrs. Coleman kept a meticulous yard, and Meredith had the impression Mrs. Coleman must sneak over to her yard while she worked because her yard had stayed nicely trimmed over the past few months, and she hadn't done a thing.

She settled Mrs. Coleman onto the swing and handed her a glass of tea. Sitting beside her, Meredith placed the tray on the side table.

"What are you doing home? A day off from the bookshop, I hope? You work so hard, my dear. You really must take care of yourself. How do you think I've lived so long?"

"I know, Mrs. Coleman, I'm trying to take it easy. I'd like to go up to Athens for the game, but I doubt I will make it."

"Oh, that would be grand. I don't know if I told you, but my dear Monty took me to New Orleans to see Herschel win the National Championship."

Meredith had heard this story many times—and had seen the snapshot to prove it.

"Mrs. Coleman, did you see anything unusual today at my house?"

Mrs. Coleman frowned and thought about the question. "Can't say I did, dear. I haven't been outside long because I had to watch my programs, and then Alexander called. And I had to do something about the dreadful state of my begonia beds."

Meredith took a sip of tea. Mrs. Coleman always had something to say about her begonia beds.

"Alexander has big issues at the law firm. Says nobody knows how to practice law these days. Says it's a shame."

Ever since the divorce, Meredith had heard about the magic of Mrs. Coleman's son, Alexander, who could do no wrong.

"I sure wish he would come here to see me. I sure think you two would be a great match."

Meredith had met Alexander once, and he seemed like Lance with a mustache and better job.

"Your gentleman caller did come around today. If you're not going to date Alexander, you should at least introduce us," Mrs. Coleman said with smile.

At almost eighty, Mrs. Coleman struggled to distinguish between the past and present and her imagination and reality. Meredith had been her neighbor long enough to know which of her stories were most likely true and which were not. But this ....

She forced the panic out of her voice as she turned back to Mrs. Coleman. "My what?"

"Your gentleman. The man at your house. I mean, I've seen him gardening, and I've seen him sneaking out the back door and out by the carriage house a couple times." She smiled and winked conspiratorially.

"You mean my former husband, Lance? The short, balding guy?" Meredith gave the most charitable description she could.

Mrs. Coleman laughed a full, hearty laugh. "Oh no, dear. Not Lance. The ... what would you say? Swarthy fellow? With the long hair. The good looking one. No offense to your husband and all."

Her legs forgot how to work for a second, but she managed to stand. "I should probably get back to the bookstore. Let me help you back to your house with the tray."

Meredith waited until Mrs. Coleman rose to her feet and escorted her home. "Thank you, Mrs. Coleman. Have a lovely day. I'll stop by later, okay?"

She left wanting to ask Mrs. Coleman a million more questions but was too embarrassed. She walked back to her house, more confused than ever.

# CHAPTER 4

When she reached the porch swing Meredith sat back down and surveyed her world. The cool breeze put goosebumps on her arms, making it feel cooler than it really was. She pulled out the ribbon, which felt like it was burning in her jeans, and stared at it, willing it to explain itself. Who else knew about *Red Ribbon*? Jennifer and Terrie. Lisa. Maybe some people in her writing workshop. And then there were the countless publishers and writers she had sent it to. It seemed such a long shot to consider them. Her novel had been submitted years ago. If it were really about the book, why would a stranger wait so long?

After an agonizing half hour, she decided to walk back to the store. Work would take her mind off her full-fledged mystery.

When she got back to the store, Nate was busy with customers. She tried to pretend it was another normal day. She called her distributors, worked on the schedule of author events, and tried to tackle the inventory. But she couldn't focus. Every loud noise made her jump, every time the phone rang her stomach did a flip, and whenever she heard a man's deep voice, she couldn't help but wonder if it was *him*.

Nate glanced at her, as he had been doing since her return. He had kept quiet, but finally broke the silence. "Anything?"

She shook her head.

Nate adjusted his glasses down on his nose in a way she hated and loved at the same time. "You've been awful quiet. Everything okay?"

"I don't know. Just a lot to take in."

"You know, maybe the police could help."

"Since when has your left-leaning ass become such a fan of the police?"

"And since when have you become a straight-up gangsta?"

Meredith laughed. "I guess a lot can happen in twenty-four hours."

She looked at her watch. She needed to get out of the bookstore but had no intention of going home alone yet. She texted her three closest friends, Jennifer, Terrie, and Lisa, and asked if they'd be open to drinks. All agreed. She grabbed her purse, told Nate she had to go, and headed out the door.

# CHAPTER 5

Downtown Savannah always reminded Meredith of Rome. She had visited Italy as a teenager, and while most cities give a sense of when they were built, Rome was like a movie without a continuity check—one era folded right into the next. With an amazing hodgepodge of internet cafes, ancient ruins, modern apartment buildings, and historic cathedrals, walking through the city was like sliding through a panorama of history.

Meredith had grown up in Savannah and made her best friends there. She went away to Athens for college—even though her hometown would always remain her favorite place, she knew it would be smart to go away for a while. She always knew unless she married a head of state she'd be coming back to the marshes. The town was small—especially during her divorce—and she was not the kind of person who found salvation in affairs and rebounds, which were impossible to hide. Instead, she enjoyed having the community's support and friendship.

Outside, waiters set up white plastic tables under portable heaters for those who weren't ready to let go of summer just yet. She passed the statue of Johnny Mercer and tweaked his nose, her little tradition that always drew at least one disapproving look—today, from an older woman with her hair fixed and set like it was 1978. Meredith smiled and winked at her, humming "Moon River," and continued on.

To her right, people lined up for Paula Deen's restaurant, The Lady and Sons. No amount of bad publicity kept them from the place, and she couldn't blame them. The food tasted monstrously good. The crowds kept Meredith away most of the time, but she occasionally gave in and ordered up a big plate of fried chicken, green beans, and cornbread. Paula occasionally came into the bookstore, and once, she even complimented her on her cherry pie. Meredith never got tired of dropping that tidbit in conversation.

Like Paula, she had found her own success with her bookstore and her baking. So why had a silly red ribbon bothered her so?

She crossed Bay Street and headed into the trees around City Hall. The area wasn't square like the beautifully laid-out spaces dotting downtown, but it took her breath away nonetheless. The Spanish moss hung heavily from the ancient oak trees, giving the city an air of mystery.

Someone broke into her house. Someone was now taunting her. Was this a warped game or a full-on assault? Should she shelve her plans and stay at the DeSoto instead?

Meredith took a deep breath and regrouped. She'd figure out those things later. If she needed to, she'd stay somewhere else for a few days. For now, Savannah demanded her attention.

By the time she passed the sinister-looking arches containing the old cotton warehouses and reached the cobblestone streets at the edge of the river, she felt more at ease. Always on the wild side, River Street opened up to day-drinking bars where tourists struggled to keep up with the regulars. It held palm readers and a dozen havens for the curio seeker.

Savannah, a city full of secrets. Ghost tours hinted at the unexplained. Civil War buffs traded explanations for the things going bump in the night. With long shadows and crisp breezes, the city felt wrapped in an otherworldly tale. She loved the feel of Savannah, a city that communed with the dark corners of history.

She walked in and out of the shops, trying to maintain the calm she found under the oak trees and working to keep the uneasy feelings at bay. She bought wine for her guests, tried on dresses, and had a glass of chardonnay at one of the bars—anything to avoid being home alone. Then the wimpy sun started to set, the wind picked up, and the streetlights turned on at once, cloaking the streets in an ancient orange glow. Normally she loved the change in atmosphere. Now it seemed too much like foreshadowing.

# CHAPTER 6

Meredith couldn't make her hand stop shaking. On the third try, she finally got the door open, only to see nothing where the red ribbon had been hanging. Relieved her friends weren't there yet, she hoped they wouldn't notice her nerves.

Her long-time best friends were regular visitors to her house. They often stopped by for a cup of coffee and a slice of pie, the radio turned to their favorite 80s station. They measured their days in coffee spoons. Meredith couldn't be more grateful for these women who had supported her through her divorce and the opening of her store, and sometimes, she worried she didn't do enough to return the favor. The difference was they had all married rock-solid guys, men who should have been her fate instead of lumpy and grumpy Lance.

After a few minutes, she heard the doorbell and walked over to let them inside.

Jennifer was a taller "twin" of Meredith with the same coloring and similar hair. She always took control. After a hug and kiss, Jennifer headed straight to the kitchen to turn up the music.

Terrie was the tallest of the three, her blonde hair cut into a pixie cut. She was the most thoughtful and the most spontaneous. She liked pearls and jeans, and her work as a teacher kept them all laughing at the funny stories her students provided.

Lisa had dark brown hair and an eternal smile. She stayed quiet while the others steered the conversation, but she was stalwart. Meredith loved to spend the occasional evening with her, sipping wine and reminiscing.

Meredith stirred her famous marinara sauce. “So, I had a little excitement today,” she said, lengthening the words to relieve their tension. “Had someone call me from *inside* my house.”

“Whaaaaat?” Terrie said.

“Yeah. Don’t know what it was about. Some guy called the store several times, and the last time, it showed up under my caller ID.”

Jennifer frowned. “You’re not staying here tonight.” She announced this as if she were the governor.

Meredith laughed. “Oh yes I am.”

Everyone offered assurances and concerns, growing more pronounced with each glass of wine.

Jennifer, who had read the scariest books outside of Meredith, acted the most worried. “Come to my house. Or get a hotel room. You can’t have possibly looked in all the places someone could hide.”

“I’ll be all right,” Meredith said.

Even to her best friends, she couldn’t tell the most important details of the day, leaving them hanging invisibly in the air. Each of these women had read *Red Ribbon*, and none understood why it hadn’t been published. So why didn’t she want to tell them?

Leaving her friends for a moment, she took some bread and plates to the dining room table, where a small packet of neatly stacked paper sat, with a binder clip clamped on the left corner. Someone had placed it in the center of the table, making it hard to miss. The words jumped out at her from the first page:

RED RIBBON
A Novel
By Meredith Harper

Her stranger had returned.

Before Meredith had a chance to hide the evidence, Lisa came into the room and quickly grabbed the papers.

She flipped through the stack while Meredith's face reddened. "What's this, Mere?"

Terrie peered over Lisa's shoulder, a smile on her face. "Are you holding out on us?"

Meredith reminded them it was time to eat and fought to get the papers back.

Lisa handed them to Jennifer, and then all bets were off.

"So you've been writing again?" Terrie had always been Meredith's biggest fan and had kept pushing her long after she had lost hope herself.

Jennifer took the pages and moved to the living room.

"The food is ready," Meredith said, trying to hide the fear in her voice.

"Dinner can wait. I think we should all come and listen to the words of our great friend Meredith Harper, who has finally come to her senses and started writing again," Jennifer said in an overly-formal tone meant to be funny.

It probably was, but Meredith felt too embarrassed to find humor in much of anything.

"It's not new …" Meredith started to protest, but Jennifer had already started reading.

# RED RIBBON

## PROLOGUE

There was a time when nothing in my life was as it seemed. Up was down, left was right, backwards and frontwards chased each other's tails in front of me. A lonely man, I buried more loves, literally and figuratively, than anyone should ever have to.

I didn't invite trouble, or at least, it didn't feel that way. Even though I was a grown man living a respectable life, I was no match for the ghosts of The Shoals, an old Georgia mansion filled with two centuries of haunted memories. It was the most terrifying and the most beautiful place I'd ever seen, enriched by the passing of the epochs. One's opinion depended, I suppose, on whether the ghosts appeared. Or if they ever saw you. I buried my truest love there and haven't been the same since. I am certainly haunted and, more than likely, wanted by the authorities. I haven't come out of the woods to find out. If I told the story, they wouldn't believe me. There are times of reflection when I don't believe it myself.

In the South, you see, ghosts are everywhere. They live in the tops of trees, call out to us in the pitch black, and tiptoe with us to our beds at night. There are the ghosts of childhood death, of raging dark anger, the angelic spirits of unrequited love. Sometimes it seems as if the world haunts the ghost instead of the other way around.

It makes sense there are more ghosts in the South; we have always borne the saddest stories. Stories of enslavement, battlefield valor, honor, and untimely death. Bigots and burdens. I've always figured that's what brings the ghosts out—the need to make their voices heard, to retell their stories. Sometimes they're warning us, uncovering danger signs long ago hidden in kudzu. Sometimes they remind us of paths long obscured by the progress of man. But mostly, I'd say, they're rolling their own personal rocks up a hill, only to see them tumble back down like Sisyphus doomed for eternity.

None of the haints I encountered at The Shoals seemed malevolent at first; they simply exhibited human emotions. They wanted attention, and I listened. Their moods changed like quicksilver, and they held grudges. I did my best to play along until my beautiful young wife transformed into one of them, living among them and becoming part of their madness.

Some would say, for sure, I followed her. I would say I didn't. I'll let you decide for yourself.

I first got to my new home in Georgia in 2009 after a disastrous time in Augusta. I had just cashed out from my startup and had enough money to live comfortably for several years. I was tired of caring about money so much. It was weighing my soul down. I missed my freedom, the thoughts of long afternoons spent in my lover's arms, evenings curled up with a good book and a tumbler of scotch. As Leah mentioned the idea of The Shoals, it sounded perfect. I wanted to work on a piece of history outside my own.

Re-doing that old house, filled with cobwebs and character and a century's worth of stories, was a chance to rewrite my own story. In reshaping that old building with my two hands, I moved a world away from the startup culture I had come to despise. I was the hero of one of those Southern tales, stirring up bones buried deep in that red clay, becoming a part of the Georgian land. My modern Georgics, if you will—all apologies to Virgil.

The Shoals had been in my wife's family since before the Civil War. People talked about it with reverence, wanting to join in its story. I played along as well, feeling as if I had walked into a dream.

The place got its name from its proximity to the Ogeechee River. It had been constructed nearly half a century before the Civil War near the then-bustling town of Washington, Georgia. Washington was a true power then, filled with antebellum homes and a generation of powerful men who would sire some of the highest leaders of the Confederacy, including Robert Toombs and Alexander Stevens. A hundred or so miles from Atlanta, now it was no longer one of the most important hubs of commerce in the state it once was. This was a sad goodbye to a storied past but another sign of the way the world had moved on. Old, sturdy storefronts closed down, and modern conveniences displaced the old and quirky. It sure seemed like a long slide from the time of The Shoals.

By the time we had bought it, the trees had enclosed the property like a green prison. Very isolated. Claustrophobic. There was a state marker there with the history of the place, and maybe a quarter mile up the road, you turned back toward the river. Our place was completely hidden and a full mile back down a bumpy road ready to punish cars.

This was not a short walk back to civilization. This was commitment and sacrifice. And we gladly chose to make it.

Often, you can see glimpses of the way things were before the Civil War. Half a mile through the dense brush are the railroad tracks, bent like an old man's spine. They were once the nervous system of the community.

The place was in the process of being eaten up by the earth. The painstaking pegged construction, wainscoting, and molding, bursting with exacting detail seen nowhere today, now was peeling and fading away. The balcony's ornate railings were angled askew or missing altogether, and the floorboards were warped. If we had given the earth another twenty years, it would devour this magnificent dinosaur without even leaving the bones. But despite all of this, the house's quality shone through. We could take it for ours and maybe save the soul and body.

I was lucky enough to do this work with my "bride and joy," as I called her. We would reconstruct it together—our forever place, destined for decades of love-making and lazy weekends away from the ever-stressful city and the silliness of man. It seemed like a dream that would extend past my middle age and comfort me as I grew old. Would I have done something different if I had known it would only last for less than a year? Or that a different location might well provide a different outcome? I can't answer that. Grief is a never-ending series of what-ifs. I've tried to move past all of that.

# CHAPTER 7

All eyes were on her. She knew it, and it caused her to freeze. The story was undoubtedly hers, but the words weren't Meredith's. Her face flushed crimson. She tried to look calm, but her heartbeat thumped in her ears. Would her friends realize how different this new novel was in comparison to the old version?

Everyone sat silent for a moment after Jennifer finished reading. The words were vibrant, and the story tumbled off the page, but those words weren't hers.

"Meredith! This is awesome. Where is the rest?" Jennifer asked.

Terrie chimed in. "You *have* been working on it! And I love it!"

Lisa looked at Meredith with an intense glare. "Seriously. Why haven't you told us? When do you have time to do this? This is really good. It deserves to be published."

Meredith didn't know what to say. Her mind raced. She couldn't tell her friends the words weren't hers … they had been left by her stalker, and she only had the Prologue.

The story came alive in this version. It sang in a way her writing never had. And her friends' praise only made her feel worse.

She officially eliminated Lance from contention in the stalker sweepstakes. He couldn't write a grocery list. Who had her manuscript and could also pull off such beautiful prose?

In fact, the writing sounded like Michael Black, an *M*, she thought. Of all the authors she liked over the years, she loved his work the best.

"Meredith." Terrie snapped her fingers in front of Meredith's face. "Where'd you go?"

Meredith shook her head and came out of her reverie.

Lisa smirked. "I'll bet you were thinking up another story to write."

Jennifer cut her off. "Or worrying about the creeper." She put a hand on Meredith's shoulder. "Please don't stay here tonight, Mere. We'll all be worried about you."

Meredith squeezed her friend's hand. "If we don't eat, the food won't be worth eating." She hurried toward the kitchen. "You go ahead and sit down."

Lisa trailed after her. "I'll help you bring things out, Meredith."

On her return, Terrie held up a wine bottle and raised an eyebrow. "If the food isn't any good, we still have this." She poured everyone a glass of wine.

The meal provided the distraction Meredith had hoped for. At least for a little while.

Lisa took a sip of wine and after setting the glass down, she smoothed the table cloth. "I cannot get the prologue of *Red Ribbon* out of my head. Where's the rest, Meredith?"

Jennifer and Terrie chimed in, wanting to hear more.

Meredith panicked. She didn't have more of the story they had read aloud. While it was her story, in so many ways, it wasn't. She had no idea how to explain. They weren't her words.

"It's not ready for anyone else to read yet. I'm still polishing it."

Jennifer grabbed the wine and topped up her glass. "Don't be ridiculous. We're your biggest fans."

She had to get them off the topic of her book. "I'm at a tricky point, and I'm afraid any feedback might cause my muse to run away." Blaming the elusive muse had worked for her in the past. She held her breath.

"We don't want to throw you off track," Terrie said. "Anything that good takes magic with a smattering of pixie dust."

Jennifer and Lisa laughed.

Meredith heaved a sigh of relief as the conversation turned to other day to day issues. Her mind buzzed, and all she wanted to do was be by herself and think. The rush she felt reading those pages provided her with more than enough courage to make it through the night. When nine rolled around, she did her best fake yawns until they got the point.

Jennifer downed the rest of her wine and rose from the table. "We'd better let our soon-to-be famous author get back to her muse." She took her glass into the kitchen and placed it in the sink. "Seriously, Mere, I'd be much happier knowing you were staying in a hotel tonight."

Meredith hugged her. "Everything will be all right."

They grabbed their things and headed for the door.

"Are you sure you'll be all right?" asked Lisa.

"Yes. I'll be fine, I promise."

"This is not some bump in the night, Meredith," said Terrie. "This is a real thing. Don't let your stubbornness get the best of you."

"What am I supposed to do? Quit living because some creep wanted to scare me?"

"No, but you could slow up a little. Give it a day."

"I'm not giving this man a minute," said Meredith. "He's not getting into my head."

It took another twenty minutes to get them out the door.

# CHAPTER 8

Meredith put on a sweatshirt and went outside to sit on her porch swing. She turned off the porch light and let the night swirl around her. Those words, telling the world she wrote them, had anesthetized her from the day's events. She felt reckless and alive; her book baby was reborn.

Years ago, she had sent the *Red Ribbon* manuscript to Michael Black. A blurb from a high profile author like Michael would surely help her get the book published, and in fact, a small North Carolina press considered it. She had no more than an inkling of his supposed interest, related to her by an assistant, but the promised letter never came and neither did the publishing contract.

She had no proof he ever read *Red Ribbon*, but the small possibility he did and liked it—despite never writing the letter—intrigued her. Could this be a strange, very dramatic way of introduction? The pages Jennifer read had the stamp of Michael Black's style. His characters connected like spirits in the night, finding their way through dark pasts to love and desire.

Since reading his books, Michael had been her dream man. He was a mysterious romantic who wrote novels about her secrets and desires as if he *knew* her. The men she had dated since her divorce were either spineless or shameless. They wanted too much, and they wanted it too quickly.

Lance, in the early years of their relationship, had been okay, but she really believed her inability to conceive came partly from a general boredom of what his offspring would be like: whiney and bland like him. He occasionally accused her of being "frigid," the unimaginative word men use to make up for their lack of imagination. She had carried the romantic torch as far as she could, but he had done nothing to rekindle the flame when the torch went out.

With Michael, something deeper stirred despite only knowing him through his books. He had touched her like no other. She used to dream he'd date all sorts of women, who would be cast aside, lacking the qualities he needed, until he wound up with her, his true love. Probably ten years her senior, he had started writing young, evolving from a petulant and talented young man to a mature mensch. His stature grew, and he became a publishing legend. Could it be possible he was finally reaching out to her?

Stuffy critics disliked him because of the popularity of his work, but they grudgingly admitted the quality rivaled the giants of the past. His *Lawton's Plan* was a stone-cold masterpiece. Everyone had a different favorite, which showed the beauty of his work. Hers, of course, was *Evangeline.*

All critics bashed Michael for divorcing his wife, Kate, who had early-stage MS, and taking up with a pretty young thing named Quinn, who seemed to be exactly as you would imagine a girl named Quinn to be: beautiful, vivacious, and utterly otherworldly. What kind of man gallivanted around the country with a woman half his age while the mother of his children struggled to get out of bed every day?

Meredith defended her favorite author online. Not an easy task. After all, who cared about his love life as long as he wrote? But then, Quinn went missing with little to no explanation from Michael. After a second interview with the Atlanta police, Michael disappeared too.

Amidst all the divisive opinions, Meredith had created Black's Legacy, an online forum for Black's fans and foes to talk about all of the theories and mysteries of his disappearance. She didn't care what Michael the man did; she wanted to venerate Michael the author—and she desperately missed his books.

Most, like her, wanted to solve the mystery. Occasionally, a true crime show aired the story, but now, five years since his disappearance, most assumed he and Quinn were dead—a twisted retelling of *Lolita* meets *Romeo and Juliet.*

All the same, she loved his books no matter what the story turned out to be. When she created the website, she had subjected herself to all sorts of mean comments and shrill invective pecked in capital letters.

Was she completely off her rocker? The man had been missing for five years. And how would he even know about her and her manuscript?

Suddenly, she remembered, and a smile spread across her face.

The porch swing creaked quietly on its chains, her mind full of books with her name on them. Every rustle of grass or breath of wind, she envisioned Michael coming out of the shadows and into her arms. But he did not come. He did not materialize out of the ether like one of his book brethren. She dozed for a moment, and when she awoke with a jolt, the spell broke. She ached for the blessed release of sleep, to surrender to her dreams once again.

Certain Michael lived somewhere in the shadows nearby, she needed to leave him a message—she understood his gift and didn't fear him. She took the red ribbon from her pocket and hung it on a plant hook on her porch. Anyone else might find it unusual but hardly jarring. But Michael would know what it meant.

# CHAPTER 9

The next few days, she stayed on high alert. Fantasy warred with fear, and fear gave way to hope. Why would he rewrite a portion of her manuscript? Did he intend to leave her name on it when he had done the heavy lifting? Thoughts crackled through her brain, giving her a jolt of energy she hadn't had since the store first opened. For the first time in years, the possibility she would become a published author allowed hope to grow.

Every day she watched for signs of him. She steeled herself for a scare, for some extra clue, for something to show herself she wasn't on the wrong path. After all, the girls asked her frequently about the strange events; she needed to be right. If she wasn't, she was in danger.

But every day, the excitement subsided. No more magic prose appeared on her dining room table. Maybe she was going crazy. But then she would go back and read those lines. They intoxicated her, kept her head above water, and made her crave more. She had no doubt Michael Black had written those words. Had he only rewritten the prologue to taunt her?

She watched her beloved Georgia Bulldogs, doubled up on store plans for Christmas, cleaned her house like a madwoman, saw friends—anything to keep her mind off the waiting.

One Thursday night in mid-October, her mysteries group met. So many people attended it was almost uncomfortable. Meredith loved this. They read Charles McCarry's fantastic book *Shelley's Heart.*

When they were done, she and Nate locked up. The night crept in earlier now, and the vibe downtown felt less like you might be attacked by a mugger and more like you might be approached by a ghost. This sounded strange, she knew, but all the same, she didn't mind having Nate to walk her to her car.

He held open the door and smiled.

She hopped in the car. "Thanks, Nate, but I'll be fine. It's not far to Drayton Street." The engine rumbled when she turned the key, and she wriggled her fingers at him in good-bye as she pulled out of the parking lot.

Meredith loved these kinds of evenings that started as a few drops of rain and a little fog and turned into an absolute downpour. She slowed down and turned up the windshield wipers. The amber streetlights flickered dimly, making it difficult to see. Luckily, she didn't need help getting home; getting to the house without being drenched was another matter.

She pulled into the carriage house and saw she had left the light on in the kitchen. Meredith frowned and wondered what else she had forgotten. The rain still poured, so she took the book she wanted to read out of the back seat and decided to wait a minute before going anywhere. Her carriage house had a newer metal roof, and she enjoyed the racket of rain hitting the unforgiving surface, one of her favorite sounds. She rolled the window down a tiny bit and took in the scene like a novelist, still hurt the promise of those pages hadn't been fulfilled.

Finally, the rain subsided to a shower. She locked the car, edged to the overhang, and made a run through the uncovered steps between the carriage house and her home. Each drop of rain hitting the back of her neck an icy insult. She moved quickly but not too fast, having slipped the winter before on a sodden leaf. She reached the back porch just short of being drenched and checked to make sure the book she had tucked in her coat survived the drips.

She stopped when her eyes adjusted to the darkness. The screen door was cracked. Her throat tightened. It had been closed and locked when she left in the morning. The breeze shifted, and the aroma of cloves wafted past.

"Michael?" Her voice squeaked. She needed the intruder to be him. She needed to understand. She inhaled deeply to help steady her voice. "Michael?"

When he answered from the dark, he took her breath away.

# Chapter 10

The heavens opened again, and rain pounded the roof and poured down the gutters in rivers. Raindrops dripped down her back from her hair, making her skin prickle, but Meredith barely felt them.

Her mouth tasted dry as sand, and she couldn't formulate words. After a few unsuccessful tries, she found her voice. "I knew you left the ribbon." She hurled the words at him like an accusation as outrage filled her. "I am so angry at you."

She clamped her lips tight and sized him up as best she could in the non-existent light.

He waited, smiling.

"I thought you'd be bigger," she added.

Michael laughed. A large, hearty, unexpected laugh. He switched on the reading lamp sitting on her porch table, which caused both of them to blink and squint for several moments.

Older than the last publicity photos she'd seen, his hair had streaks of silver running through it and had grown longer—the pony-tail length of Mrs. Coleman's description. The gleaming, intelligent eyes that had drawn her in from his first book jacket still called to Meredith, and she wanted to sit down beside him. She should call the police, but part of her wanted to invite him instead.

"You scared me to death," she finally managed, like a teacher scolding a headstrong student.

"I'm sorry if I'm a little unorthodox," he said, trying to wipe the smile off his face.

"Unorthodox? You broke into my house! And made threatening phone calls!"

Unfazed, Michael shrugged. "I gave you a mighty nice gift." He said it matter-of-factly like he usually skated on his mistakes by presenting lavish literary gifts.

"You gave me a wonderful gift, but I don't understand it."

He shrugged. "I tinkered. I fixed. I thought you would like it." His eyes held a small apology.

She wanted to accept. "Of course I love it. It's not your writing that scares me, it's your tactics."

His eyes flared, and his lips curled into a snarl.

Meredith took a small step back.

At her movement, the jovial Michael returned as if the other had never existed.

"Why did you do all of this?"

"I wanted to make sure you liked it," he said, "before I made my proposition."

# CHAPTER 11

Another drop of icy water ran down her back. She shuddered. "I have to get dried off before I catch my death."

Meredith opened the porch door and walked inside, firmly shutting the door in his face and turning the deadbolt. She toweled off her hair and slipped into something warmer. When she returned, Michael was inside the door, a sheepish grin on his face.

Before she had a chance to scream, he held up his hand.

"Please, let me explain." He touched the package firmly clamped under his arm.

She pointed a finger at him. "Don't move. If you so much as take a step, I'm calling the police." The package he carried must contain the rest of *Red Ribbon*. Meredith desperately wanted to read what he had written, but she didn't want to be the victim of the weirdest home invasion on the planet. She quickly opened the windows to let in the sound of the rain—and to let out the screams if anything went wrong.

"All right." She faced him, hands on hips, glaring. "Explain. I want to know why you're doing this to me, what your *proposition* is, and where you've been all this time."

He gazed into her eyes. "What I have to say might take a while. Do you mind if we sit down?" He motioned toward the couch.

She gave a short nod. “I’ll get us something to drink.” She hurried into the kitchen and leaned her head against the pantry. What on earth was she doing? Mock headlines flashed through her mind. *Savannah’s Premier Bookseller, Meredith Harper, Invited Her Slayer in for Tea.*

She needed some sort of weapon … just in case. She couldn’t exactly count on being able to inflict injury with hot tea, and Michael might react badly to her walking in with a carving knife. Her eyes lit on the unopened bottle of Merlot from when the girls had been over. She’d be able to inflict some damage with a corkscrew.

She grabbed the bottle of Merlot, the corkscrew, and two glasses, and made her way to the living room. She sat in the upright chair opposite the couch where he lounged and laid the corkscrew within easy reach on the table after pouring the wine.

Michael picked up a glass of wine and glanced at the corkscrew. “You don’t trust me.”

She arched her brow. “Should I?”

Outside, the rain beat against the house.

He paused for a moment, eyes focused on the wine in his glass. “I guess I deserve your distrust. I thought a little mystery in your life might be appreciated.” He raised his gaze to meet hers. “I know you want to hear the story. So unless you stop me, here goes.”

Michael took a sip and set the wineglass on the table. “An emotional young woman, someone I never should have become involved with, became increasingly unstable, and one day, she left.”

“Quinn.”

He nodded. “I thought I knew her, but I had barely scratched the surface. That’s about as simple as I can make it.”

“I like simplicity. But her emotional instability didn’t mean you had to disappear.”

“You’re right.” He wet his finger and ran it around the rim of the wineglass, making it sing. “But truthfully, I didn’t want to go back to

Kate. I know I sound like a horrible person, but she was difficult to live with *before* she got MS. She turned the kids against me. Never could get them back. I knew the press would eat me alive if didn't go back to Kate. I couldn't handle the drama, and I sank into a deep depression. So I disappeared."

"So are you 'coming back' now?"

He laughed. "Hell no! It's been the best thing I've ever done. Life is simple and kind."

"So what are you doing here?"

"There's only one thing I miss."

She knew what he would say. She saw it in the way he dropped his eyes and then looked up expectantly at her. "Writing?"

He nodded. "That's part of it. But actually the whole process. Writing, getting published, the readers. Seeing others fall into my stories and them telling me about it."

"And you can't do that if you're dead."

"I thought about dangling a manuscript out a couple of years ago, but there was still so much attention regarding the disappearances. I figured better safe than sorry."

"So what is this?" She pointed to the package sitting next to him. "What's the proposition?"

Michael gave a lascivious look. Then he smiled. "It's not really a proposition," he admitted. "It's not mine; it's yours."

"Is it … different?"

Michael laughed. "Pull it out. Take a minute. I'll excuse myself and use the bathroom." He looked at her with a twinkle in his eye.

She moved to the couch and flipped the reading light on.

# RED RIBBON

## CHAPTER ONE

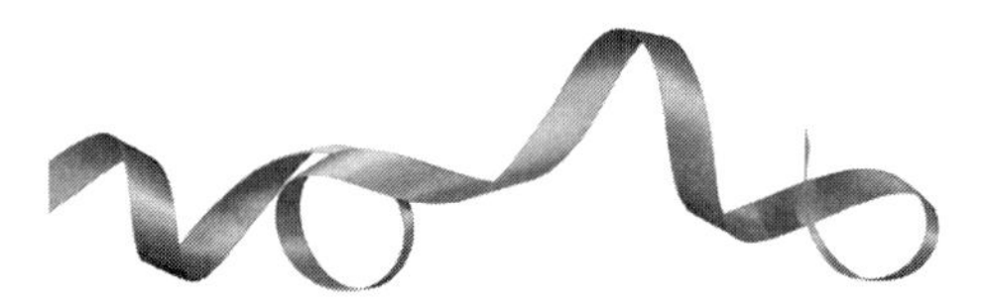

Leah was an impossible combination of passion and common sense. She was a realist, bordering on pessimism in her daily decisions, but her energy was so strong it seemed as if the whole world moved at her command. To have her on your side was like having a tribe of wild angels doing your bidding—you knew you couldn't lose.

She had been my rock during the time I considered leaving the website. The money was getting scary big, and I was out of my comfort zone. I wasn't built to run Fortune 500 companies, and despite the fact we were maybe eighteen months away from buying-Caribbean-islands kind of rich, she didn't complain when I wanted to walk away. She reminded me I was walking away with more money than all four of our parents had made in their entire lives—probably twice as much. With plans to move to the country, we would never have to work again if we didn't want to. She said she could think of a lot more interesting things to do with our time.

Leah was passion personified. She lost herself when she made love and was unapologetic for the sounds she made and the curtains she ripped. She kissed deeply; she bit; she scratched. She had a look that reminded me of past passions and alerted me to future rendezvous. I've never seen that look in another woman, no matter how fierce the connection. People wax poetic about what they would give to see someone smile or taste the salty essence from a lover's neck, but they tend to inflate what they would give up to have that feeling one more time. I'm lucky to have that one more time look in a few of the photos she let me take, ones I had to develop myself because her nakedness—the magnificence of her body, the perfect curve of her breasts—was the least intimate thing about them. I have never shown anyone. Not once. I never exposed her, not even after all the strangeness that was to come.

Leah was the one who initially suggested The Shoals. The property had been in her family for generations and was owned by an uncle, one who was perpetually in need of money and not particularly interested in the history of a dying plantation. We bought the place for $20,000, which was a steal even if you razed the mansion and just rented the place out for farmland or sold the timber. It was a beautiful structure with good bones despite its weathered condition. There were no houses for a mile in any direction, and we fantasized about wild summer parties with people spilling out on the lawn, cocktails, loud music, and dancing until sunrise.

There was a moment that first evening we saw The Shoals together, holding hands in the absent-minded way we always did. It had rained earlier that day, and our appointed walk through had been postponed until late afternoon. The place was sticky and hot when we arrived, the cobwebs heavy with dust. The wood buckled and creaked under our footsteps. I turned to her and was struck by her beauty and the gentle way she tilted her head to look up at me.

"So, when are we moving here, Rhett Butler?"

I grinned. "This is a long way from an Applebee's, you know."

"My point exactly! Authentic culture! Bootstraps! All the things we say we long for!"

I shook my head, knowing she had me. "Let's do it."

Leah kicked her heels up and squealed. She smiled at me in a way that let me know she had always known we were going to do this but also said she was very happy I agreed.

The clouds had moved out, exposing a late-spring Georgia sky, the wet green of the grass, and the sight of a woman beaming with laughter and life. It was a forever moment, one where the word isn't spoken because it's utterly unnecessary. We stood there for a long time, both of us taking in what this decision meant. I looked at her and thought of what she meant to me: permanence, stability, commitment, and desire. Most men never find all of those qualities in the same woman. I had.

She moved next to me and toyed with the buttons on my shirt. She bit her lip and caught my eye.

"Got that blanket in the car?" she asked, knowing the answer.

The sun bathed her face in a mix of soft oranges and yellows. She looked like a movie star and gave me a soft, expectant kiss.

Luckily, the car wasn't far away.

I spread the blanket on the porch, which looked more enticing than the muddy ground. When I rose from bending to spread it out, she kissed the back of my neck. I almost turned to meet her lips, but something stopped me. This was her moment. She wrapped her arms around my chest, her breasts pushing into my back. Looking like a nymph of summer, she turned around to face me and whispered in my ear.

"You will never forget this day."

And then, like a storm rolling in over a foreboding sky, she kissed me firmly on the lips and dug her nails into my back. She bit my cheek so hard I thought she had broken the skin. Leah stepped back, smiling, waiting to see my response. I grabbed her and pressed her against me, fully aroused, and bit her lip so hard I was afraid she would bleed. She didn't. But she took me with a fury I hadn't ever seen. It didn't take long for both of us to reach the heavens and tumble back to earth. We lay there, half-naked, soaking in the old house and the wet Georgian dirt and hoping it would be that way forever.

I couldn't wait to move to The Shoals.

# CHAPTER 12

Meredith didn't realize she had been holding her breath until she finished reading the chapter. This was her novel, and yet, it wasn't. She flipped ahead quickly, scanning pages to see what changes were ahead. The characters and plot were generally unchanged, and yet, the reading experience couldn't be more different.

The book read like a Michael Black novel. These characters had their own, distinct voices. They came to life on the page and felt real. And at that moment, she realized how silly it had been for her to ask for this man's approval.

Meredith looked up to see Michael filling their wine glasses. "I don't understand."

He joined her on the couch. "What's to understand? You had a great premise. It just needed some work."

"This is more than just some work. "

"I enjoyed the challenge—fitting my work into someone else's plot. I'd never done it before."

Meredith's head swam. She didn't like wanting to forgive him so easily. And yet, there it was. The manuscript lay there on her lap. It had her name on it. "What am I supposed to do with this?" She waited breathlessly to see what he would say about the million-dollar question.

"I told you. It's yours to do with as you wish." Michael inched closer to her.

His eyes were hard to look away from but harder to meet.

"You can put it in a drawer and keep it hidden away, or you can give it to the world."

She looked at the manuscript, then at Michael, and then at her glass of wine. She grabbed it and drank it too quickly. "Why did you call it a proposition?"

He waved her off again. "A bad joke."

"I need to read it first."

"Of course." He grinned at her.

The manuscript burned in her hands and begged to be read. She wanted to return to it, but she wanted to hear about this man's journey to … where? The rain kept up its steady cadence, punctuating their discussion with thunder and the occasional damp breeze through the windows.

Her initial anger receded, replaced with a sense of wonder and curiosity. Here stood a man the entire world searched for. Yet he didn't go to the New York City literary lights. He chose to be with her, looking at the seashells she had collected, and begging her to partner with him on a novel. *Her* novel.

"Why me? You have many defenders online. Ones with better-known sites."

"There are many *whys*, but you are far lovelier than any of them. When I saw your site and put two and two together with the manuscript, you were the obvious choice."

She frowned when he mentioned her looks. It temporarily broke the spell the manuscript had woven. "Is this just some sort of elaborate scheme to get in my pants?"

Michael smiled. "What would you say if I answered yes? A grand romantic gesture—the gift of literary immortality for the momentary pleasure of your bed?"

Meredith blushed. She remembered some of the passages of his books, ones as familiar to her as Bible verses. "I'd have to say it was the nicest invitation I've ever gotten."

"Would you consider it?"

She frowned again. "Is that why you did all this for me?" She held up the manuscript like a rare vase.

He winked. "You're a beautiful woman. Let's just say tonight isn't the first time I thought of it."

"Well, you tell me, Mr. Black." Meredith moved her body slightly but with great intent. She twirled her hair in her hand, something she hadn't done in decades, and made him wait on her next words. "Is this a great novel?"

"This novel by Meredith Harper is a good one." Michael looked at Meredith.

His eyes burned into her, and this time, she couldn't look away.

Then, just as quickly, he dropped his gaze. "Go and read it and decide for yourself." He stood up slowly. "Now, where am I sleeping?"

She folded her arms and clutched the manuscript. She wasn't expecting him to be so blunt, but she realized she might as well get used to it.

Michael picked up on the hesitation. "I've just given you the greatest gift of your life. You can at least give me shelter for the night."

She wanted to be more forward than she had ever been in her life—to step towards him and dare him to kiss her. But she stayed in place. She smiled big enough for both of them. "The guest room is all yours."

But the smile faded. She remembered the strangeness of the porch. He seemed to know how trusting and accommodating she would be. She wanted to be contrary and not so easy to read. But she felt intrigued and aroused, and she wanted to get back to reading. Despite her trepidations, she led him to the guest bedroom.

# RED RIBBON

## CHAPTER TWO

We disengaged from other activities and started spending more time at The Shoals. We braved the increasing heat and marveled when flowers opened and trees bloomed. The pines didn't change, of course, but there was enough in bloom around us to make the adventure that much more real. We brought sleeping bags and had a routine, one which allowed for a couple of hotel stays each week in Washington or Thomson. We learned how to talk to the locals and get their approval for our adventure. Of course, we didn't need it, but it meant for a whole lot less interference when everyone felt like they were a part of our reviving of a town jewel like The Shoals.

I learned to ask questions, sometimes knowing the answers, at hardware stores and town diners. Early on, Leah and I agreed we would not be secretive or standoffish. "Everybody wants to be a part of this," she said, bringing up a point I had never considered. "They may not have the money to refinish an old home, but they'll be happy for us if we just don't act like assholes." I loved that side of Leah, sidling up to Dan Kirkland or Ronnie Johnson at the grocery store and flirting just enough to see their interest change, filling them in on all that was going on at our "country spot" as she called it. I reminded her we no longer had a "city spot," but she was unfazed.

I needed her, because I was overwhelmed. The work was so much more physical than anything I did previously. I pulled my back the second day of the strenuous labor and felt every twinge of the next week's work trying to get it to heal. She had her own long list of tasks to accomplish, but she found time and energy to make me forget my pain. We were in the woods and alone and made a daily ritual of long, almost spiritual sex. My other relationships had sex as a component, but Leah met me on every level. I never had to apologize for wanting her, never had to schedule ecstasy. The way we breathed, the way we talked, the glances we shared in the company of others. It was all a part of that connection, spurred by a smell of her perfume or a Roxy Music song. It was a union so special I knew and felt it at the time, never having to be reminded by anyone else. We didn't complete each other in the sense of a Hallmark card; we just existed on another level, with no thought of how others existed. We were special and perfect together.

Those evenings, that summer, too many to number, too marvelous and precious to catalog, now are the bedrock of my memory, my nightlight. The world changed, but my allegiance to that universe never will. It will be mine forever.

And then, one day, Leah found a letter.

One afternoon, as she was cleaning out some built-in bookshelves, Leah noticed a letter sitting up top, wedged next to the wall. It was an old letter from bygone days, in a script both beautiful and very hard to read. It was yellowed and torn, and the writing seemed to fade off the page. We made out it was written, most likely, by a woman whose name was C, but the letter wouldn't yield any more secrets. It was too faded and delicate, and no matter what light we brought to try to decipher it, we agreed we had gotten no further.

Working on a house in the condition of The Shoals, especially knowing the evening would mean I would taste my lover's sweet body yet again, meant each day felt like a penitentiary sentence. Time dripped like an old faucet. I found myself gazing into rooms and thinking about objects—what they meant and how significant they might have been in other lives. We understand the earth-shattering moments, when the

Civil War comes through your front yard, when we all watch the towers fall together, but the constant connection to life and change is really where the moments live on. Births and deaths and calm nights in. Days turning into years, turning into lives lived. I was determined to live that purposefully with Leah. Each day was a potential paradise. Why waste even one?

Maybe a month into our serious pursuit of conquering The Shoals, as I waited for the evening's bliss and my constant quest to learn the details and mysteries of the place, I examined the absolute wonderment of the detailed, ornate woodworking pattern carved into one of the fireplace mantles, all flourish and intricacy, painstaking and vibrant. How much had we lost, I thought, when we lost that level of beauty and richness in every detail and left it all to computers. Every day seemed like a new vote for The Shoals Life, as we took to calling it. But that day, I heard an angry, distressed sound. One I hadn't heard since coming to this place.

I turned around and moved to the window. Something caught my eye outside.

It was Leah. She was downstairs on the lawn. She was furious, and I opened the window to see why. I almost called out, but something kept me quiet.

"You're wrong," she said, emphasizing the word. "You're wrong as you can be."

I struggled to see with whom my wife was arguing. Did I need to go downstairs and help? But I couldn't see anyone. The lawn was empty, the forest beyond quiet.

She sat there, still in reverie, lost in time.

"Leah?" I finally called out, unable to take any more of the mystery. "Who's there?"

Leah did nothing for a moment and then finally turned to look at me. She found my face in the window and smiled, seemingly happy for me to break her concentration. "What do you mean, honey?" she asked.

"The person you were just talking to," I said, confused.

She looked left and right. She turned back to me. "What are you talking about?"

I didn't ask her any more questions about it. But the scene unsettled me, and her face, normally my personal Rembrandt, now came to me wearing that sad, harrowing frown.

# Chapter 13

Meredith read well into the night. The sounds of Michael rustling around in the guestroom came through the walls, but after a little while they silenced. It had been so long since she had read a new book by Michael she had forgotten the sheer pleasure of it—the sense of dread in the narrative, the atmosphere, the fullness of characters. Then she corrected herself—this wasn't a Michael Black book; it clearly said *Meredith Harper* on the first page.

Reading the book humbled Meredith; it showed her what her manuscript lacked and the deep chasm between good and great. And the story, although she knew where it headed because she had envisioned it, seemed new and fresh and thrilling. She awaited each new page.

Yet, she had to consider so many things. A big part of her wondered why he didn't simply come out of hiding and announce he was alive and writing again. If he didn't do anything wrong, he shouldn't have anything to worry about. Which made her wonder if he *did* have something to do with Quinn's disappearance. The breaking and entering and strange stalker stuff didn't speak well about his mental state.

But the worried side of her worried lost the battle to the romantic, hopeful side. She had created this frame upon which Michael had hung his masterful canvas; her name would be on the spines of great books;

and most importantly, she couldn't deny she was in love with him.

As she read the romantic scenes between the unnamed narrator and Leah and watched the glimmering promise of their early relationship fade away while madness slowly replaced it, Meredith found it difficult to stay in bed and not go to Michael. She hadn't slept with anyone since Lance, but that part of her life had ended and it took everything she had not to open Michael's door.

But a small voice kept her in her own bed. It reminded her of the real and practical concerns—Michael Black had hidden from the world for years, and many people believed he murdered a young woman. The thought kept Meredith in her own room—at least for the time being.

# RED RIBBON

## CHAPTER THREE

My wife didn't really descend into madness. In my mind, descending implies a time element, a slow and steady journey. Leah plummeted. Careened. She occasionally reemerged, sometimes even held her head above the water for weeks on end, rejoined me in the caresses and the wonderful feeling of deep knowing we had about each other. I've thought about this often, wondering if any clues predated the lawn incident, but I can't remember anything that so much as hinted at the hell to come. But if there were any questions about how much things were changing, she introduced her new side to me—and to the rest of the town as well—on June 22, the summer solstice.

We planned a party to show off The Shoals. It wasn't close to being done, but by then, we had put enough into it to stay there without a tent, which we considered a major victory. We called it The Before Party and gave everyone invitations to The After Party to be held on the same date the following year.

Amazingly, the weather cooperated. The days leading up to the party were long and warm, only hinting at the blazing temps July would surely bring. The brightness of the days promised to delay the darkness well into our festivities, and the magnificent evenings, when the sun seemed to hesitate just before setting, are now a part of my forever memory, the last moments of the old regime. That was the time of the forever love, and that week we treated The Shoals like a free love commune, brazenly and openly falling into each other. Leah had a look, playful and brazen, that seen in any situation meant her clothes were coming off and, most likely, very soon. I tried to meet her in passion and creativity.

The night before the party, knowing a catering truck would be coming, I kissed her hard and heavy right on the front porch, which was surely blushing by then from all of the craven sexual acts we had performed. I grabbed her hair and put my finger in her mouth. She playfully held my neck and choked me and told me we were going to play a game.

She took off the blue sundress she wore, the color of a cornflower, and I saw she wasn't wearing anything underneath. She shoved me down to the floor of the porch and told me I wasn't to talk. She took me in her mouth and looked up at me, a hint of merriment in her eyes. She took the head of my penis, so delicate and sensitive and sucked on it only, nothing else, until the sensation of that threatened to make me explode. She did it so long and so hard, laughing as she enjoyed my pleasure and pain, that I just couldn't stand it. She finally, after one more playful tug, let me loose, to realize how aroused and hard she had just made me. She lowered herself onto me, then tickled me with her hair against my cheek while she gave me the slowest, most intimate moment I can remember.

It was poignant and perfect until we remembered that guests might come at any minute. My mind immediately went to the embarrassment of being caught in the act, but Leah dismissed my concerns. "If they come, let them enjoy the view. Maybe they'll want to join in."

My wife was a freak, and I made up my mind I should enjoy it. I held my ground and finished up the most full-body orgasm I had ever had. And as we went inside to re-clothe, I heard the van coming up the drive.

The next day promised to be even better. Everything was planned and grand. I picked out the music and decided to make it an all-Georgia playlist. I pulled tracks from R.E.M. and Otis Redding and mixed them in with The Star Room Boys and Michelle Malone and Drivin' N' Cryin'. We bought long strands of old-fashioned Christmas lights, flickering in blues, reds, and greens, and strung them into a large circle of pines. Leah bought dozens of citronella candles, and I bought pounds and pounds of shrimp for the grill. Our front yard had transformed into an oasis like something out of a storybook—the happy couple who broke away from the kingdom and found everything they desired. I had the most beautiful woman in the world, one who adored me and pleasured me and made we weep with joy and emotion. Why wouldn't I celebrate this moment? Why wouldn't I want it to last forever?

The evening filled with laughter and stories, the languid breeze, music, wine, and the perfume of early summer. The cicadas, frogs, and calls of summer birds joined in, full of song and warm weather promises. The color of the sky undulated from a soft, gentle blue into a color scheme that challenged people to find words to describe the loveliness. The darkness eventually drained the colors away, leaving the stars, out in the middle of nowhere with none of the city's ambient light, providing the last, and maybe best, show.

Our friends, who trickled in from Athens, Atlanta, and the nearby towns, were blown away. They ate shrimp and drank white wine and told stories. There are nights you're where you're supposed to be and doing what you are meant to do; that was one of those nights. I enjoyed showing my new life to my old friends and meeting new ones. We all waited for Leah, who had run into town for some last-minute reinforcements.

It was getting late, so I tried calling her. Cell phone service was never great at The Shoals, but I wanted to make sure she was okay. No answer. I chalked it up to Leah's perfectionism.

I saw her before anyone else. She was driving way too fast over the small hill. People had to jump out of the way. Then she crashed into one of the pines, the front of the car crumpling against the tree's ancient truck. Christmas lights came tumbling down, turning the oasis into an accident scene. She leaped out of the car and made a bee-line for me.

"What is the meaning of this?" she screamed.

I assumed she was screaming at me, but it seemed equally aimed at anyone at the party.

"Where are they?" she asked, again, scanning the crowd.

Her friend Penelope tried to approach her but was given such a withering look she withdrew.

"Where are they?"

I didn't know what to do. I tried to approach her and comfort her, but she spit in my face. She muttered something incomprehensible. It wasn't English. It was scary. People eased away. I wiped the spit off my face and reached my open hand to her, but she fell to the ground and sobbed.

"Biggest mistake of my life, biggest mistake of my life."

I felt carved out. Everyone left quickly except for a handful of my Athens friends and Matt and Penelope, the only friends we had made in our short time in town. Penelope went back over to Leah, who was now in a heap, and rubbed her back and asked soft, soothing questions. Matt and I went and looked at the damaged vehicle. I offered apologies and got the expected, "Don't worry about it." My Athens friends helped me carry in the full coolers of wine and beer. The few ladies from town still standing at the corner of the house looked at me and drew straws trying to figure out what I had done to that poor girl.

After I had busied myself all I could, I walked over to Matt, Penelope, and Leah. She was sitting up now, holding a beer and looking lost. She looked up at me and, with sad, pleading Leah eyes, said, "I'm sorry."

She stood up and offered her arms. I held her tightly and led her to the bedroom. I let her climb into bed and then went out to apologize once again to Matt and Penelope.

"Do either of you know what that was about?" I asked.

Both shook their heads.

I came inside, dreading what was going to happen next. I noticed the old letter out on the table as if Leah had been deciphering it again. I shook my head and put it away. There was nothing else to find there.

# CHAPTER 14

The sounds of someone rustling around had been in Meredith's subconscious for a while. She woke up and saw a beam of light coming in her window. She took a second to lay back and realize Michael Black must be making those sounds. Oh how many people she would like to tell. She closed her eyes and pictured him moving around her kitchen, half-dressed and hair tousled from sleep. The fresh aroma of brewing coffee seeped under her door. *Time to go downstairs*, she thought.

She bit her lip and tried to decide what to wear. Fully dressed? No. Cute PJs? Seemed contrived. She decided on a Georgia t-shirt, some plaid pajama bottoms, and a pair of slippers. She checked her hair to make sure it looked reasonable and walked downstairs.

There, on the coffee table, sat a beautiful bouquet of fall flowers: dahlias, chrysanthemums, and lilies—an arrangement you might see at a nice hotel.

She couldn't breathe.

Michael stood over the kitchen counter, beaming.

"What are these?"

"Pretty sure they're flowers."

"I wouldn't know. I never get any." Lance, always the practical one, had given her flowers maybe three times during their marriage.

He moved toward her, and his smile reached his eyes. "I hid these in the garage last night. Figured they'd keep. I am not always the best communicator, but I wanted to say thank you. For everything you've done for me—defending me, sharing your story with me, and sharing your home."

Meredith gave Michael a big hug, wishing it were more but resisting. As hard as she tried to hold back the tears, a few had already leaked out.

Releasing Michael, she stuck her nose right in the flowers. Then she took it all in, looking up at Michael and his smile, and breathed in the sweet smell of the moment.

Had she ever had such a morning? Filled with promise, her favorite books, and a handsome, smart man?

# RED RIBBON

## CHAPTER FOUR

The party gutted me. Not only because Leah's actions were so out of character, but because I felt like she left me looking stupid as well, and made it look as if I had been anything other than a terrific husband. I have never been one to seek others' approval to any great degree, but there's a difference between looking for attention and opening one's self up to ridicule. Since I hadn't seen all that was to come, the jarring change in Leah was heartbreaking. Every nod, every slight, made it seem as if I had done something wrong, when all I continued to do was love that woman to the ends of the earth. Imaging waking up one day and finding your best friend no longer spoke the same language. That was life with Leah as the disease spread.

We both began to find other interests—ones that tied us deeper to the land and pulled us farther away from each other. I focused on the history of the plantation and the stories and artifacts buried just below the surface. Every morning, I would take my metal detector out into the woods, wave it though the long grass and creeping vines, and wait for the machine's hurried rings to announce any treasure.

Those moments were zen for me, helping to connect me to the place. I felt it would help Leah as well, but her effect was practically catatonic, and anything I asked her to do, any connection I tried to make, was met with indifference (on good days) and, completely new for Leah, scorn and ridicule. It was like watching a fine cathedral being demolished by a wrecking ball.

My main interest in the metal detecting, of course, was the connection to the Civil War. As far as I could tell, it was still practically being fought in these parts, but more than most places, we had a direct and provable connection to that conflict. The Shoals had been used as a hospital for the invading Union Army during the Civil War, and some of their scribbles and graffiti on bedroom walls had ended up in museums. A major general in the Union Army, Judson Kilpatrick, stayed in the house during Sherman's march through Georgia.

Everything made more sense once I learned that history. It pained me greatly to realize I wouldn't be able to share in the excitement of the discoveries with my best friend. She told me in no uncertain terms she couldn't care less.

Even the ghost stories seemed to spring from the 1864 march to the sea, and many touched on his right hand man, the disgraced Kilpatrick. The more I read and the more I dug, I stood in awe that one event could create so much disturbance, so many lasting ripples. Of course, at the time, the area was overrun by outsiders with no loyalty to the land, and many abused the ground along with the people who called it home.

One of the more popular stories was about a beautiful young woman from a well-known family who disappeared, leaving a loving husband and two young children behind. It was thought she was cheating on him. Months later, they found a Northern soldier, the last person seen with her, wandering through the woods in a bloody uniform. The man refused to speak, and they couldn't officially connect him to the disappearance of the woman, but the locals always thought they knew the truth.

There were many other stories of rage, longing, and loneliness. I was convinced it was the blood that had turned the Georgian clay red. From time to time, there were still retellings of these stories by people who were sure they accounted for everything from unexplained noises to genuine madness.

I thought about this and the changes in my darling wife. Was the land causing her drastic diminution? That seemed outrageous.

I bought the most obnoxiously expensive metal detector I could find and every conceivable accessory. Leah couldn't stand this new hobby of mine, but as I bought them, I thought of the way she looked at me with such disdain in front of everyone at the party, how her eyes accused me of crimes I had never considered and couldn't name. I bought maps and magazines, and I commandeered the dining room as my workspace.

At that time, too, I wasn't the person I became either. I longed for an apology, an explanation, some sort of affirmation of what I meant to her. I longed for the simple act of healing. But as nothing remotely resembling that came my way, I foolishly hardened my heart.

I decided to start my expedition in the backyard. I had recently run into Matt in town. He was supportive but full of warnings. I waved him off, impatient for discoveries.

"You'll find some cool things. I don't have any doubt about that. But just remember there's a lot of rough history in that place. My grandpa told me the peg construction they did on your place would have taken slaves at least five years to build. That means there were lots of people around. People living, and people dying. You're just as likely to find a skeleton in that place as you are a scabbard."

I started on a particular spot around a clump of overgrown hedges that caught my eye. Leah was in town doing some shopping, so I knew I had several hours of privacy. You had to be so intentional to come to The Shoals. There was no happening upon it. It was so completely returned to the wilderness you could look for it and still miss it.

That first day, it didn't take me long to hit something. It had rained the two nights before, and the dark Georgia clay was soft in my hands. I carefully broke apart the wet clods of dirt, feeling with my fingers for something foreign. Then I found it—a buckle. Too small for a belt, too large for a shoe. And the angle wasn't square, either. Nice find for a new guy, I thought. That was enough. I wanted to head back inside and see if I could figure out what it was.

But before I stood up, something else caught my eye: cloth of some sort. It was tucked underneath the buckle and took a second to loosen. I carefully tugged and pulled and worked on the area around it. Then it became clear; it was a lady's glove, still maintaining a bit of its charm despite being caked in mud for well over a century.

That note of delicacy, that sense of connection, almost startled me. My heart leapt, and I felt an odd and strong connection. This was what I was looking for. This was the exhilaration I needed. What story did it hold? How was such an ornate and beautiful thing cast aside and buried in the earth?

The glove was amazing enough, but I could feel something inside it. My heart raced faster as I realized what it was: a letter similar to the one Leah had found, or so it seemed.

Surely, Leah couldn't turn this down. Certainly, she couldn't scoff at something so personal and intimate. Maybe it could even bring her closer to me, instead of the inevitable tectonic shift that daily sent us farther apart.

I sprinted back to the house, hoping Leah would be there. My anger towards her momentarily dissipated in light of the discovery. When I reached the house, panting a little, Leah wasn't back. That disappointed me, but I wouldn't do anything with the letter until she came back home.

I carefully set both items on the counter and waited in giddy anticipation when someone knocked at the door.

I thought about not answering, but I realized it might be Leah; perhaps she had forgotten her keys. That wasn't like her, but who knew what the new Leah did with keys. Before I could get there, the knock came again.

"Hold on. I'm coming," It had to be Leah.

It wasn't Leah. I opened the door and saw something almost out of a painting—a lovely young woman. Lovely didn't do her justice. Delicate and pale and blonde with a plain white dress and a red ribbon in her hair. She stared at me as if I knew her. But I couldn't have forgotten anyone so achingly beautiful.

# CHAPTER 15

"How did you sleep?" Michael asked as he made Meredith breakfast.

Just some pancakes and bacon but so alien for a woman whose most romantic history had been the occasional trip to Lowe's with the hubby.

"I'm afraid my nomadic ways make it difficult to sleep in a new place," Michael said, massaging his neck.

Meredith wanted to flirt, but she couldn't figure out how to get back in the swing of things. Instead, she went the practical route. "I'm sorry you didn't have much to work with food-wise. I cook more at the bookstore than I do here."

"I meant to mention it to you." He put the finishing touches on some scrambled eggs. "Your store really is wonderful. After all, it has every one of my books." Michael laughed loudly.

"When did you come into the store? And how did I miss you?"

"You wouldn't have thought to look for me. I've been in there a couple of times over the last month."

She frowned. "How long have you been staying in Savannah?"

"Just a few weeks before I reached out to you." He looked down and shrugged like all of this was normal. "Since I finished with *your* novel."

Meredith wondered how much she wanted to know the answers to the questions she asked. Meeting this man had certainly been much more than she expected. "Where have you been staying?"

"Not far." He nodded in the direction of the historic circles, where there were plenty of nice hotels.

"Any chance you did a little reading last night?" he asked hopefully.

"Just some new work by my favorite author," she said playfully.

"You mean yourself?" He grinned and said with mock surprise, reaching out to tap her gently on her forearm.

"I haven't finished yet, but this experiment has undoubtedly shown me the difference between good and great."

"Thank you," he said.

She expected him to needle her, to tell her she couldn't have done it without him. Instead, he made her a breakfast plate, seemingly doing anything to avoid eye contact.

"Why did you use my novel? You never seem to lack for a good plot."

Michael scratched his chin. "I have plenty of other ideas for books, but disappearing can get pretty lonely and I thought perhaps I should take on a pupil."

Meredith's heart raced. To be a student of the great Michael Black would be a dream come true.

"Quinn's father and those deputies put me through the ringer. Wanted to charge me with murder. It's not going to go away."

"Where have you been?"

"All over the place. There's a couple of old biddies who are big fans in Lausanne, Switzerland, so I spent a fair amount of time there. It's easier to blend in when I'm out of the country. I've spent more time than I care to in Europe."

"Come on. I'm sure the disaffected act works with some of your ladies, but it sounds pretty fabulous to me."

"Just not my cup of tea. I like the way we mix it up over here. But there are a lot more people who know my face here, so it's easier to stay hidden abroad."

"You're pretty good at it. I mean, your biggest fan missed you, two times, in her own store," she said.

"You were busy. You've got a business to run."

"Still. Makes you wonder how vigilant we actually are."

"Why don't you stay home and read today." The beginnings of a smile peeked out from behind his coffee cup.

Meredith wanted to burst into song. A day off from work with her favorite author would be heaven. Her staff could more than handle running the store without her. She grabbed her phone and texted Nate.

> Hey. Having a skip day. Can you believe it? Need to catch up with some things. The place will run fine without me, right?

She put the phone back down and returned to the table with a smile. "This feels like hooky. I haven't taken a day off in a long time."

"My whole life feels like hooky," Michael said. "This feels real to me."

Meredith pushed the hair back from her face and tucked it behind her ear. "I'm flattered."

Michael took the dishes to the sink. He turned back to Meredith. "Why are you here by yourself? Why haven't you found someone else?"

Meredith stood and shook her head. She met him at the sink and stood a little too close to him while he finished washing. "I'm not interested in 'someone else.' I want the right one, or no one. I'm happy where I am." She met his eyes to make sure he understood.

He looked away. "I'm sorry," he said, flustered. "I didn't mean it like that. It's just you have so many great qualities."

Meredith looked puzzled. "Oh, but you've just met me. I'm sure a ton of people would tell you otherwise."

Michael let her have the sink, and moved toward the living room. “How far did you get last night?”

“Not far enough. I wanted to read more, but I fell asleep.”

“Where did you stop?”

“Not long after the embarrassing summer party.”

Michael raised his eyebrows. “So not to the rainstorm yet?”

Meredith searched her memory. “No.”

Michael winked. “You’ll know it when you get there.” He smiled again.

Her cheeks heated at the thought of the rainstorm scene. How much more steamy would he have made it?

She cleared her throat to hide her embarrassment. “Are you glad you went into hiding? I still have to say I don’t really understand why you did everything the way you did.”

“You haven’t had detectives following you to the drug store,” he said. “You haven’t turned a corner and watched the man ahead duck back down the alley. They didn’t have anything on me, but I really believe if I had stayed around, they would have arrested me anyway.”

Meredith shook her head. “They’d never take you in—unless there was a body or evidence you … did something.”

The sound of the text message startled her. She looked down.

```
Nate: Sounds great. Enjoy it!
```

What would he think if he knew she was having breakfast with Michael Black? He was a fan as well but more skeptical about Quinn’s disappearance. He would be worried to death. She looked back at Michael as he continued.

“That’s the problem,” Michael shot back. “I don’t know there isn’t one. Quinn wasn’t old enough to be a stepmother or to deal with a bitter ex-wife. I should have known and never brought her into the situation.

But I don't know she didn't … do something rash."

Meredith shuddered, picturing a lovesick, half-grown child alone and desperately seeking Michael's love but not knowing what to do in his grown-up world. She had to admit it was not the most far-fetched possibility.

"I've read the message boards. The dad despises you."

Michael nodded and lowered his head. "I'd probably feel the same in his spot."

"I debated him once or twice, but it seemed crass on my part. I can't imagine his pain."

Michael nodded. "At first, I wondered if they were just looking for money. But they don't need it. It's just a good, old-fashioned quest for justice."

"Well, from what I heard, you did quite well with your last contract with Gandolfo-Griffie."

He smiled. "I don't ever have to worry about money. And my secret guru has done me good during my sabbatical. I've got more money now than when I pulled this little stunt."

"It's good to know being on the lam from authorities won't break you."

"You know, I didn't live extravagantly. I still don't."

"I know what the press says. But Michael, I don't really know you."

He looked angry for an instant, and then his face softened. He moved a step closer. "You know me. You know my books. You know my intentions. Maybe better than I do myself. I've read your website."

She looked up and caught his eyes. They were mysterious, the color of obsidian.

He chuckled, breaking the tension in the air, and then turned his attention to the bookshelf in the corner. "So, what are you going to do on your big day off?"

"You know what I'm doing. I want to finish your book. And after all, it's not every day you get to meet the great Michael Black."

"You want to see it through to completion, huh?" A corny line, but it worked.

She stammered and hated herself for it. "I am just so honored to have the great Michael Black in my humble abode," she said, bowing and curtseying. "I hope he enjoys the privilege of being with me half as much."

He gave her a flat look she couldn't read.

"Michael is enjoying his privileges," he said.

He held her every emotion as he gazed for longer than she wanted. Then he gave her a half-cocked grin; the gesture mattered far more to her than it should.

# RED RIBBON

## CHAPTER FIVE

The woman gasped and nearly jumped when she saw me at the door. I was clearly not who she was looking for. I think she wanted to run away, but the house was so secluded there was no easy move.

She fumbled around for a second.

"Hi," I said, embarrassed by how badly I wanted to impress her. "Can I help you?"

She stood there for a second, rubbing her hands like they had a stain. "I … I … believe I'm in the wrong place."

Maybe she was there to see Leah?

"Were you expecting someone else?" I volunteered.

She shook her head and started to walk away, still wringing her hands. "I'll find my way back," she said.

I walked her out, impatient to get back to my discoveries. But when she left, I felt an emptiness in my stomach I didn't think I would feel after I was married. This stranger meant something to me. I went back to the kitchen, still not feeling quite right.

Who knew how long Leah would be gone. I couldn't wait forever. My discoveries were calling to me, so I decided to pick at the buckle first. After looking it up online, I was convinced it was some sort of boot buckle from the Civil War period. I imagined the officer who might have worn it and how he lost it. My head dreamed up all kinds of scenes—from battlefield valor, to it falling off unnoticed, to illicit battlefield couplings.

I went down the rabbit hole, painstakingly examining my find, considering its meaning. I was so far down I didn't even notice Leah when she finally arrived.

When I looked up again, I saw Leah peering over my shoulder. I had been so lost in the research I hadn't even heard her come in. She looked genuinely interested. The mood was so good I decided to skip the story of my visitor. Instead, I told her about the glove.

I touched her face and kissed her, hoping that genuine, white hot passion would return, and Leah would again be my wife in all senses. She kissed me in what I could best describe as polite. It was not going to lead to unceasing passion.

But she was interested in the finds, even despite her protestations. She held the buckle and turned it around, taking a moment to admire the handiwork. She paid careful attention to the glove, memorizing its details and was as much in love with it as I was. After she finished her inspection, she pulled the letter out. It felt much like the other one, dry and dark yellow, with dark brown markings that seemed to scream its age and connection with the war. Leah beamed. I grinned. That spark reappeared for a moment, like a breath we shared, as we waited to know what connection we held. But, sadly, it didn't take flight. Not like the old days. Instead, we stared at the letter, determined to understand this missive better.

Best as I can remember, here is what it said:

*Gen. K – I know you ask for more familiarity, but this is the best I can do. I am treading in unusual circumstances. To ask for more is more than I intend to give.*

*Do you think they know? They are acting strange. He won't open up enough for me to be sure, but I fear their knowledge may be more than what we had counted on.*

*As for your other question, I do not know when we can meet again or where. Last time we were nearly found out. I think a face-to-face meeting would be much too risky now.*

*Yours truly,*

*C*

I say "as best I can remember" because the words lasted but a second before our eyes. Before we even knew we needed to commit them to memory, they were gone, except for that same confident C.

# CHAPTER 16

Meredith went back upstairs and started reading. Her breath slowed, and she fell back into the plot. Chapter Six saw another violent outburst from Leah, one which put her in the hospital. Just as she finished the chapter, she heard a paper being shoved underneath her door. She smirked a little as she retrieved the note, covered in the same angular hand.

*Meredith:*

*Confession time.*

*I have found you intoxicating for the better part of a decade.*

*I know it sounds crazy, or maybe even creepy, but after you sent me your manuscript, I watched you from afar. I should have taken a different approach, helped you get published, done something more direct, but I was still entangled with Kate and Quinn and didn't want to knock you out of your pristine existence if I couldn't promise any more than drama and intrigue. I didn't want to meet your husband for fear I would like him, and I didn't want to meet you for fear you wouldn't like me. And then my life dried up into its own ghost story with the law waiting behind every corner.*

*I am out of touch and out of practice. I am making that clear and up front. But I reached out from the great beyond to take this chance. If I seem strange, it's because I want to impress you.*

*You are a night in May. Your smile is a new language I want to learn. It is hard for me to write about you when I actually know so little. I haven't touched your lips or felt your embrace. It is easy for me to slash with words, to frighten, even to excite. But writing something I mean is a whole different encounter.*

*Forgive me. I'm out of practice. But I want to learn.*

*M*

Meredith went back to reading, trying to stop the pounding of her heart and the soaring dreams enveloping her. Then, after thinking about it, she let those dreams fly for a minute.

# RED RIBBON

## CHAPTER SEVEN

It seemed to take forever to get home. The rain came down in sheets, and I slowed the car to a crawl. The car's radio hadn't worked since the crash the night of our party, but the rain would have drowned the music out anyway. My heart felt like a plane that could no longer fly.

The passionate, vibrant woman I had married had completely decompensated within half a year. I had heard the death in her wails when I entered the bedroom last night, the sadness melting into the madness.

"Why did you do it? Where are they?" she repeated, over and over, her voice dripping in sorrow.

Outside her window, the storm raged, and there she was in a shapeless long gown, praying to an unnamed list of angry gods, hoping to find redress from the heavens when everything on earth seemed to be collapsing.

Everyone wants there to be a logical answer to that sort of madness. If only mental illness was simply a puzzle to be solved. If only Leah could be put back together. I still loved Leah, but she was incapable of loving back.

The never-ending drive back home, dark and so heavy with rain and worry, relentless and scary, every few feet another possible treacherous skid into the ditch, left me tense and tired, depressed beyond my expectations, alone with my worry. My spirit, so nourished at summer's arrival, so buoyed by the promise of what we were all about, now seemed hidden in the dense and unforgiving forest. I was stripped of hope and almost as demoralized as whatever was left of my dear wife. I needed a spark, a jolt, some light in this unceasing darkness.

At home, I went straight to the kitchen and poured myself a glass of bourbon. It burned my throat and hit my stomach hard and heavy until the numbness I craved blissfully arrived. I chased it with another for good measure, desperately praying for some sort of oblivion. I saw the kitchen knife beside the sink and, for a moment, could almost feel the knife cutting ribbons into my wrists, just a momentary pain, waiting on the relief that would surely follow. I even touched the handle, toying with an idea I knew I wouldn't really consider. They say vertigo is not the fear of falling but the fear of jumping, and there was a minute when I was on that proverbial roof, almost ready to take the ride. But I knew I would hold on, wait until I might see some promise in another morning. I dragged myself upstairs, so heavy with dread that turning on the TV we had recently added was too large a task to hope to complete. I touched the remote and felt heavy. All that I longed for was deep, semi-drugged sleep. Sweet oblivion. It was just moments away. I climbed under the covers with all my clothes still on. The pillow smelled like Leah, and something about that earthy scent opened me up like a pig to slaughter. I cried like I never had. I was alone in the middle of Georgia with no family and few friends. My wife was unknown to me. I had considered leaving this mortal coil. Even the house seemed to weep around me.

Rain led me into sleep. Its cousin thunder awoke me.

I awoke to the loud crack of lightning. The sound shook the glass in the windows, and I worried there would be fire. Then another crack of lightning, this one as bright as a June day, and the room lit up. That's when I saw her, standing at the foot of my bed. Her white dress was soaked through, sticking to her body.

Catherine, the beautiful girl with the red ribbon in her hair.

She slowly pulled her dress off over her head, revealing her beauty. Was I imagining this? Was this some sort of sick joke from hell? Or was it simply that a beautiful woman was offering me something Leah had long stopped being capable of giving?

I wish I could say I was racked with guilt, but the truth is stranger. Catherine's appearance obscured the memory of my wife as if Leah, her beauty and her slide, was nothing but a dream I'd once had long ago.

I motioned Catherine to my side of the bed. She walked over slowly and sat next to me, her eyes watching mine all the time. Her body was damp and cold. She took my hand, caressed it, and looked deep into my eyes.

I reached up and untied the red ribbon from her hair. Her thick golden hair slid down her neck. Suddenly, this woman meant everything to me. I kissed her, first nibbles and then something more, coaxing her into joining me. All my fears and regrets, all my loneliness, confusion, and anger about Leah, the house, my life—it all slid away like the rain dripping down her body. Time went off its stern and ever-vigilant watch and left us to our own instincts.

I put my hand on her shoulder and kissed her again, lowering her into bed. I cradled her head and began to kiss her for eternity.

Her breasts had that light taste of life itself. The taste of her made me young and innocent again. I lifted up each breast, searching for the creases where no one touched, and kissed underneath them. I pulled her to me, caressing the skin stretched delicately over her ribcage like ridges on the edge of a china plate. Then my thumb traced the spaces between, and I noticed a scar, about an inch long, ran parallel. Although fully healed, I looked into her eyes and told her without words she was safe with me, her and her secrets. I moved my head down and kissed her scar gently. Even her imperfections were beautiful.

The rain crescendoed. It whipped against the old glass, but the house kept the outside at bay. I pulled her closer and kissed her lips until I felt I knew her gentle soul.

I reached down to touch between her legs, her pubic hair soft on my fingertips. She shuddered when I touched her, and I understood I would be her first lover.

Then she reached for me, her breath hot on my neck. In a single moment, she changed from naïf to vixen. She pushed me flat onto my back, her arms pinning my shoulders to the bed. I smiled. Ever the man, I assumed I had the power. In that one gesture, I realized it was she who owned me.

We didn't speak that night, not when we found a rhythm and both held on, not when we interlaced our fingers and climaxed together.

Before we fell into a deep and velvet-sleeved sleep, I noticed another scar about the same size and age on her right shoulder. It gave me pause, but I feared breaking our wordless reverie. Instead, I ran my finger along its surface, and she kissed me, and I forgot all about her secrets, and we fell into each other, utterly spent.

I awoke suddenly. There was a ghostly quiet. The storm was gone. I could hear the insistent beat of my heart, the way Poe might have described it. I turned and saw she was no longer there. Her pillow was still damp, and I buried my head against it. I missed her terribly. I needed to gaze into her eyes in the morning and play gently with her hair. The warmth and completeness my body felt before was gone. I was cold and alone. The shame threatened to explode in my chest.

What had I done?

# CHAPTER 17

Outside, the rain beat steadily. It hinted at the approaching change of season and the shortened days ahead. A perfect day for reading.

The chapter had made Meredith swoon like a teenager watching Elvis for the first time. Meredith always experienced a lesser degree of this bliss any time she read a new book by Michael, but the circumstances, in her case, had turned a dull longing into full blown arousal.

It had been over two years since Meredith had last slept with Lance. She had woken him up in the middle of the night, climbed on top, and took him in a way she never had before. She wanted him to make her feel good, just once, and she wanted to use him like he'd used her all those years.

Whereas Lance's attempts had been purely physical—impatient hands grabbing for her belt, turning her around, and bending her over the counter on the few occasions he showed any desire at all—Michael's writing focused on the intellectual connections people developed as lovers. A dance drawn by circumstance and desire but not always commitment. Michael's books were not about convention but about the edge of life, where indelible memories were made in an instant and sometimes tragic moments changed things forever.

She felt the need to burst out of the room and bare her soul to this strange man. But first, she really wanted to finish the book—*her* book.

# RED RIBBON

## Chapter Ten

Catherine came around again the next day. She clearly had some way of knowing when Leah wouldn't be around although we never talked about her. I was upstairs working and was glad to see her walking up the driveway, the red ribbon especially bright on a gray day. I walked downstairs and gave her a big smile. She would have come to me, but she bore a gift, a pitcher of tea. It seemed odd to imagine her carrying a beautiful piece like that for a long distance, but I was happy to see her and not interested in playing detective.

I invited her in, but she declined. She kept her eyes down, and it wasn't until I sat down on the porch with her that she had anything to say at all.

We sat with the silence. In a way, it seemed natural. Our evening, so full of passion—it was hard to imagine what to say.

She finally broke the silence. "You shouldn't be alone all the time."

I had no answer for that. I didn't know if she meant in general or she was blaming Leah for the strangeness of the past few months. I said nothing. She poured me a glass of tea, and I tasted it. It had notes of lavender and something that reminded me of plum. It was unlike any tea I'd ever had. But it felt warm, and it was from Catherine, so I loved it.

Finally, I brought her up, attempting to say what I needed to say about her without ruining my rapport with Catherine.

"You know, I love her but hate who she has become."

"I know. I felt that way once myself."

"It's just she's ..."

She reached across the table and touched her finger lightly to my lips.

"You have put yourself in a lonely position. It would be easy to fall into madness. You don't have to apologize for loving her. But I won't apologize for loving you."

Catherine turned slightly as if determined to leave the conversation behind.

She looked up at the second floor. "I have always admired this house," Catherine said, with a faraway look in her eyes.

"There's a lot to do, but yeah. It's a pretty special place."

"You can see all the way down to the river," she said, almost to herself.

I was confused. The trees were too thick to see all the way down. I wondered if she'd confused it with the view of her house.

Now I was intrigued. "Does your house have a view of the river?"

Catherine put down her tea and looked straight at me. "There are things you don't need to know. I am able bodied and perfectly willing to come over here. Isn't that enough?"

I held up my hands in mock surrender.

"Would it change the way you held me last night? Would it change how I want to care for you?" Her face was pained.

I had again pressed the wrong button. I wanted to head for a retreat. "It wouldn't change my feelings for you at all." It felt strange to say that as a married man.

"Good." She put her hand on top of mine. "I love taking care of you." She smiled sadly.

I looked into her eyes, needing answers.

She gave me none.

# CHAPTER 18

Meredith loved *Red Ribbon*, although it had ceased to exist as something she created. Yes, there were moments where her words shone through, but his manipulation made her manuscript so much richer. She wanted to plow through, but she reminded herself to savor, not devour reading Michael Black. Meredith decided she needed a break, so she headed downstairs to feed her curiosity over her mysterious guest.

She found him sitting on a stool at the kitchen counter, a blank stare on his face. She was slightly disappointed; she had expected him to go into her extensive library and pick out an exotic companion.

He looked up, surprised, and took a second to collect his thoughts. "How did I handle the rain scene?"

She pursed her lips. Was the book all he thought about? She didn't answer right away. She went over and looked through the fridge, pouring a glass of orange juice. "I approve. In fact, I approve of everything. Especially the letter."

He ignored the comment. "Where are you now?"

"Just past there. They've just had tea."

Michael moved closer to her. He reached out to touch her forearm.

Out of instinct, she pulled back. She didn't mean to, and her face flushed.

“I’m sorry,” they both said at the same time. They laughed awkwardly.

Meredith waited a second and then said, “I’m gonna get back to the book.”

A look of annoyance flitted across his face but was gone within a moment. “Good,” he said with a smile she didn’t believe. “I’ll be right here.”

# RED RIBBON

## CHAPTER TWELVE

The next find was my favorite: an old pitcher, nearly intact, found not too far from the main place I had been digging. I was fairly certain I had stumbled on an old trash site, a great find for someone looking for relics.

The china pitcher was decorated with a pretty gold and blue flower pattern, still vibrant and mesmerizing. Besides a chunk missing from the bottom and a couple of nicks at the top, it was in perfect shape.

I hustled in the house and showed Leah, who was doing her best to be more accepting of my treasure hunting. She ran her finger along the side of it and remarked on its beauty. She asked if she could copy the designs for an embroidery pattern or as inspiration for a tattoo. This was "better" Leah—still not back to before but trying to be supportive, to be a good partner. She didn't say it directly, but I knew she was trying to make amends for the hell she'd put us both through.

I worried constantly she would relapse and feared she would stop taking the drugs, since they dulled her mind. Even in a moment like this one, where she tried to play the part, I knew there was a constant back and forth to return to who she once was. She needed that vibrancy and light, but every day with "better" Leah made me long for the original that much more. I compensated by being overly cheery and eager to please, always pretending like everything was normal. She was kind enough to play her part in the charade.

Of course, I never mentioned Catherine and the odd and delightful times she showed up and passed through my life like a beautiful dream. I rationalized. I cried. I made many resolutions. But in the end, I was faced with the realization that I had honest feelings for two women. The fear in meeting someone new, I found anyway, was not the losing connection with the first woman; it was the odd and completely unsettling sensation that you loved them both.

The upheaval inside Leah made my shifting allegiances easier. We couldn't touch romantically; the doctor said she wasn't ready for that. On her "lesser" days, her nightmares and paranoia kept her apart from me. The demons still lived within her. She was just better at keeping them hidden.

I knew so little about Catherine. I had only the vaguest ideas about where she stayed when she was in the area, and she seemed so out of place with her unwired lifestyle. Speaking with her was refreshing; she was always attentive and rarely distracted, not neurotically comparing herself to other women. Leah had always been constant nervous energy, moving from one crisis to the next.

I carefully cleaned the pitcher in the sink with warm water and soap; Leah supervised over my shoulder. I looked for distinguishing marks that might hint at its age or type but found nothing. It reminded me of Catherine—timeless and elegant.

Suddenly, there were knocks at the door, sharp and insistent, startling both of us, and the pitcher almost slipped out of my soapy hands. I froze. The only person who ever knocked and didn't use the bell was Catherine, but the knock seemed different. I couldn't breathe.

"I'll get it!" Leah smiled and headed for the door.

*Dear God*, I thought. What am I going to do?

# CHAPTER 19

The doorbell rang and interrupted Meredith's reverie. She hurried downstairs, and Michael, a wanted man, headed up the stairs, giving Meredith a worried glance as he passed. She motioned for him to keep moving.

"Just a minute!" She checked the mirror before opening the door.

Standing in the rain with no raincoat, no umbrella, and flowers in his arms was Nate. Meredith's heart sank. But before Nate sensed her disappointment, she lit on a plan.

"Nate!" She opened the door with a grin fit for a hero. She maneuvered him inside, ignoring the bouquet. "What a surprise. Who's running the store?"

"Jenny"—a mother of three young children and the wife of an overbearing husband worked at Southern Gothic sporadically but enthusiastically—"came by and said she needed the time away from the munchkins." Nate's clothes dripped water onto the floor.

"I feel like a bad parent or something not being there. Anything interesting happen?"

"Yeah, one thing. An older woman came in. Seemed nice enough and everything. But she swore she saw Michael Black in our store a few days ago."

Meredith stopped breathing.

"Said he had a pony tail and kind of salt and pepper hair."

She started breathing again. Nate didn't believe the woman.

"Said he asked about you."

"What did you tell her?"

"I think she was a little tipsy." He mimicked a drinking gesture. "I wanted to tell her Wilkie Collins and Arthur Conan Doyle were today's guests."

"Nate!"

He chuckled to himself, very proud of his joke. This gave him enough confidence to hand the daisies and purple mums to Meredith.

It looked as if he had picked them by hand.

"I brought you these," he stammered, his cheeks glowing.

Meredith saw her opening. "Okay," she said, her face like a drill sergeant, convinced she could handle this. "Shoulders up and chest back."

Nate looked at her in horror.

"Whoever this lucky woman is who will be getting these flowers needs to know you mean business." She put the flowers down on the counter and came close to his side, putting a hand at the base of his spine and using the other hand to pull his shoulders back. "Everything this woman needs to know about you should be able to be said without any words—simply by the way you look at her, the way you stand, the way you touch her." She looked at him and winked, hoping later he would appreciate her saving him from embarrassment.

"I don't know whether this is the girl you talked to me about a couple of weeks ago, but I'm so glad you stopped by before you dropped by her place because you're getting this all wrong. You need to take the lead, not come in mumbling and apologizing. Obviously, you didn't *speak* an apology, but your body language did."

Nate looked gobsmacked. "An apology?"

She nodded. "Go in there like you own the place. There's nothing sexier than confidence." She thought about the man overflowing with confidence upstairs.

Nate dug in deeper. "What are you—"

She handed the flowers back. "These are beautiful. She will love them."

He wasn't going to make this easy. "Would you want—"

"Nate," she said gently, "I have a date tonight." The words almost caught in her throat.

"Anyone I know?" he asked.

Meredith hesitated before answering. She knew Nate loved Michael's books. "I don't know. Perhaps you've seen him around town," she said. "I think he's come into the store once or twice."

Nate lit up. "Elvis. He finally came back. Or Ambrose Bierce. He's been gone longer. Or no. Something *you'd* like more. I've got it. Michael Black!" he laughed.

Meredith's eyes grew to the size of Japanese lanterns, thankful the joke had given him an out. He could leave with his dignity intact.

His mood brightened, and he walked out the door but then turned back. "Meredith?"

Already heading upstairs, she turned around and met his gaze. "Yeah?"

"Thanks. I appreciate all the help. Have fun tonight."

Meredith certainly hoped she would.

# RED RIBBON

## Chapter Thirteen

Leah had almost reached the door. I hurried toward her, preparing what I would say to both of them.

Leah cracked the door, and a figure pushed it open with such force it threw her back and caused the door to pop against the wall. Light flooded in, and for a moment, I couldn't make out the visitor. Slowly, he came into focus. He was a wiry man clothed in a denim shirt and light-brown dungarees. His hair was jet black, and he had a handlebar mustache. I had only a second to size him up. Maybe this was a hipster get-up. I wasn't sure. He was certainly true to the character if it was.

He stormed through the room, radiating a menacing energy from his pores. He stopped just in front of me, his body vibrating with anger. He wasn't tall, but he didn't have to strain to be menacing. He sized me up and then pushed the words up out from his belly. "Mr. Cheely, are you the one? Are you the dog who defiled my wife?"

"I think you've—"

"Answer the question!" His face was inches from mine—so close I had to manage everything I had not to move into him.

"I'm not Mr. Cheely."

He relaxed and took a step back. He smoothed his shirt and looked at Leah, who was panicked. I worried about what effect this would have on her.

"He's not Mr. Cheely." She shook her head and repeated.

"She said it was the plantation owner." He looked confused and was losing steam.

"Plantation?" Leah looked confused. I shot her a look telling her to play along.

I shook my head. "I'm sorry; I'm not Mr. Cheely."

The man turned and looked directly at Leah, his face turning a deep shade of crimson. He turned back and looked at me, sizing up where he had gone wrong. Finally, he turned to Leah and said, "I'm very sorry, ma'am."

There is no man more dangerous than a disgraced husband. I couldn't imagine what it would feel like to lose Catherine, and my heart was still adjusting to the scar of losing Leah. I didn't relax, unsure what the man's next move would be.

He turned to me as if he could read my mind. After a moment, he nodded. He slowly backed out of the house until he was halfway down the front path and then turned and sprinted down the road as if his fury required a more fulfilling confrontation.

Tucked in his waistband was a wood-handled large caliber revolver. I fell to my knees. My world was careening.

# CHAPTER 20

Meredith went back upstairs and found Michael had gone into her room and closed the door behind him. Part of her hoped to find him lying in her bed, but instead he stood at the big bay window, watching Nate's car back down the driveway.

"What did he want?"

He sounded jealous.

"He works for me at the store."

"I saw him too. Does he fancy you? Do you fancy him?" He turned to look at her, his face creased and sour.

"We are not in the 1800s. I think that's the last time people 'fancied' each other." She tried to lighten the mood. Michael had been carried away like a character from his book.

"Why did he bring flowers? You're sure getting a lot of them lately."

"Why are you in my room?"

"I'm sorry. I picked the wrong door." He spat the words out.

"Seems like you do that a lot. Oops! Forgot to get an invitation. Let's just break and enter."

"Maybe I picked the wrong pupil." He glared through her.

Meredith tried not to look hurt, but the comment struck her right in the gut. She had no answer.

"Look," he said, "if I'm interrupting some budding office romance, I can leave any time."

She fidgeted with her hair. She hoped she could walk this back. She didn't want Michael to ruin the mood the book had created.

"I told him I had a date with someone else."

"Well, am I in the way then?"

Meredith took a deep breath. She looked at the silly man. "Look. I don't know what that boy did to piss you off, but if you think I'm interested in a skinny, little kid barely out of college, then you know a whole lot less about women than I've spent the last twenty years giving you credit for. I came up to ask you where we were going to dinner, but if you insist on behaving like every other man I've ever had the misfortune to meet, then I'd rather go read *my* book and be alone."

She slammed the door, her hands shaking, and walked downstairs for the manuscript. Her knees only wobbled slightly, or at least, that's what she told herself.

# RED RIBBON

## CHAPTER FIFTEEN

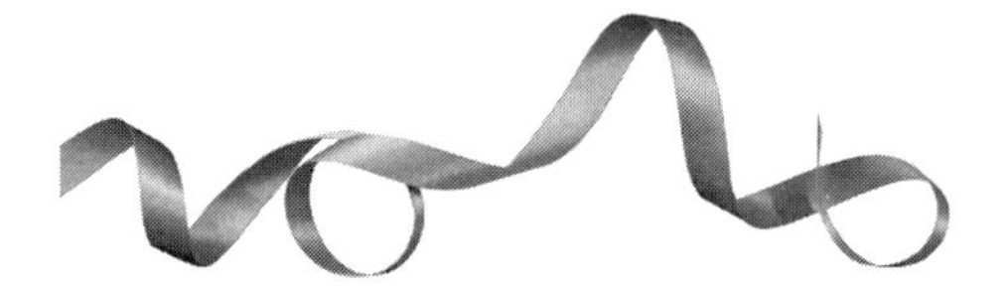

That winter, the weather felt cold and desolate and rivaled a good northern one. The north Georgia wind cut right through me. The countryside turned snowstorm gray like a winter without Christmas. The sky was the color of my mood every day Catherine didn't return. Other times, when a storm whipped up, it reminded me of the turbulence of still being connected to Leah, a constant tension in the back of my mind that trouble could come at any moment.

Catherine, as you would expect, hadn't been back. Perhaps we were both afraid of what her husband would do to us if he learned the truth—that he was wrong only in my name. As weeks turned to months, I dreaded his return less, and despite the feelings I still had for her, I grew used to the thought I'd never see her again.

I tried to focus on Leah. With winter on top of us, it was good her condition was improving. But without the promise of Catherine's return, that seemed as cold and empty as the unfinished rooms in our ice water mansion.

The house was much closer to being finished. At this point, we focused on more detailed smaller projects. She took to the painful detail work involved in breathing life into a home of a certain age—restoring the woodwork, sanding the molding, varnishing the built in furniture. She got good at it, and I did my best to be gentle and encouraging.

Slowly, Catherine's porcelain beauty began losing its power over me. I started to feel more shame about my affair and deep regret over breaking the commitment I'd made to my wife. She gave away nothing to hint that she knew, but we were still so out of sync I had trouble reading her, and besides, Leah was so untethered I often wondered what she really remembered about our halcyon past.

No new letters emerged.

I decided the best thing to do—in addition to trying to make friends and ease our entry into the community—was to learn more about the history of the place. By this point, I was doing it for me, but I hoped I would get to see it through. Both of us wanted things for the house that had meaning. We wanted everything to be from the right era, and to the extent possible, we wanted each item to have a connection to our home. Truthfully, it was a great excuse to get out of the house, go into town, and spend a few hours by myself at the library, surrounded by books and far away from Leah's painful silences.

The history of the place extended further back than Kilpatrick and the Civil War. The Shoals had originally been purchased by a Revolutionary War hero named William Bird from Pennsylvania and Benjamin Hamp from Georgia. They bought thousands of acres, hoping to build mills on the property. They wanted to put the mills close to the site where the house was, and when they finally built the woolen mill, it was believed to be the first of its kind in the state. Colonel Bird and his family moved nearby, and their house was known as The Aviary. It was located across the river from where The Shoals would eventually stand, and their family graveyard remained. Colonel Bird was buried there in 1812.

Thomas Cheely, Leah's distant relative, bought the place in 1812 and added a grist mill to the thriving woolen mill. He built the house using peg construction during the early 1820s. It was expensive and time-consuming, taking the five years Matt had told me about, even with slave labor.

In the war, Georgia didn't see as many battles as border states like

Kentucky, Tennessee, and Missouri initially. But later, to break the Confederacy, Sherman made his famous march through Georgia. There was no denying the people's allegiances; after all, he brought Georgia out of a gauzy dream and reverie and into the nightmare of a war fought at the front door. It destroyed homes and broke the spirit of the people, much like those people had already done to generations of slaves.

The Shoals was directly in the path on one side of Sherman's two-sided plan. General Kilpatrick, who was fresh off losing a part of his command after a disaster in Richmond, and his soldiers used our house as their headquarters. Kilpatrick spared the house and the women, but he ordered the mills to be burned. I tried to imagine the scene—the women and children must have been terrified the fires engulfing the mills would overtake the house as well. I could almost smell the smoke and feel their fear.

Was this land cursed? Was it going to swallow Leah and me up, too?

The history was interesting but constantly depressing. What crimes and what joys had taken place here? What else did the property hold? How did it relate to my wife's fragile psyche?

Again, after another helpful period, Leah dove back into the murky darkness. She was back to the insults and name-calling, and sometimes, it seemed she fought people I couldn't see. That much pain starts to be hard to understand. We cycled through more hospital visits, and Leah's desperate pleas to avoid them only made it worse.

We still attempted to be normal. She would occasionally try to be lovey-dovey against the doctor's orders, but for me, that ship had finally sailed. It was like cuddling with a wooden box. Leah wasn't there anymore. I struggled to find a name for this stranger I shared my house with.

We watched *Raintree County*, a late fifties Elizabeth Taylor movie about the Civil War. She moaned and complained and made watching as uncomfortable as everything else we did. I told her I was going to bed early. I didn't mention anything about being very mad as I assumed it wouldn't matter to her anyway. I poured myself some whiskey—something I noticed myself doing more frequently—and laid on my side of the bed. Within seconds, I was in a black cocoon of sleep.

Then I awoke with a start. I don't know how long I had slept. My wife was standing over me, all shadows and breath, inches from my face, trapping me in bed. She was moving back and forth as if dancing to music only she could hear. One hand moved in toward me and then away as if casting a spell. Her eyes, those lovely jewels that had first drawn me to her like a siren's call, were now full of hatred and madness. They stared straight through me.

In her other hand, she held a sharp long kitchen knife, the one I had touched while thinking of ending it all.

I surveyed my surroundings in an attempt to plan my next move. I pushed myself back from the brink of panic. Did she know about Catherine? She moved the knife over my chest, mimicking the movements that would drive the blade into my heart. Then she caressed it, fondled it, even ran her tongue over it. Once, she lunged at me with it, and it took every ounce of self-control I had not to jump up and grab the knife and subdue her. I had heard stories about people who under the power of their madness have a supernatural strength, and I did not want my life spilling out onto this floor, which now seemed like it was made of curses.

She moved back by two or three steps, and her silent tarantella grew grander. The dance was beautiful and strange, and she was like a voodoo queen, wild and enchanted. I realized the woman before me was a stranger, a creature distant and alone and utterly different from the person I had married. I knew sleep wouldn't come that night. I wondered if it would ever come again.

# CHAPTER 21

Meredith went outside and sat on the porch. The air smelled sweet with the aroma of clove cigarettes, and it reminded her of the first day she found the red ribbon. Since Michael's arrival, her life had filled up with so much meaning and intensity.

With the rain's steady drone, the porch proved to be the perfect place to continue the novel. She hoped heaven was like this—calm, temperate, and full of porch swings. This porch had sold the house. If it were socially acceptable, she would live on the porch and rent the house to someone else.

In the backyard, there were four trees laden with Spanish moss. She watched the water drip down the tendrils of moss, a mesmerizing sight. The trees were easily a century old, probably older.

Southerners always found comfort in their version of history—genteel kings and queens of a republic never allowed to flourish. Meredith knew this wasn't true; there were more bloody graves than mid-summer parties under the live oaks, but those myths nevertheless enchanted her. She prayed for something to keep her tethered to the life she knew and to help her rebel against this dream spinner. But what would life be if she couldn't follow a majestic dream? The thought of having her name on this book was almost more than she could stand, even if Michael didn't know how to behave around a woman.

When she read, she left her earthly surroundings behind. Her breathing slowed. Her shoulders relaxed. She succumbed to a gentle hypnosis, especially when conducted by the master—and herself. Reading these pages, she fell back into her own dream.

When she looked up, she saw Michael approaching. She bit her lip to hide her smile. He looked contrite, holding his hands like he was apologizing to the sheriff in an old western.

"I'm sorry," he said. "I should have known you wouldn't be interested in that pipsqueak."

Meredith frowned. "That pipsqueak is my friend." She saw the crestfallen look from Michael. Maybe he retained a bit of sensitivity after all. "But I'm not interested in him. I'm afraid I'd eat him for lunch."

A corner of Michael's mouth turned up. "He might like that." He cringed. He had missed his mark.

Michael was so rusty at this whole flirting thing. Then she remembered how hard it would be to completely uproot from family and friends and become utterly alone. Plenty of women would still find him attractive, if he wanted, whether they knew of his literary past or not.

"Will you take me to dinner tonight? I'm just going to ask since you keep screwing it up."

He laughed. "I'll think about it." Then strode back into the house.

# RED RIBBON

## CHAPTER SIXTEEN

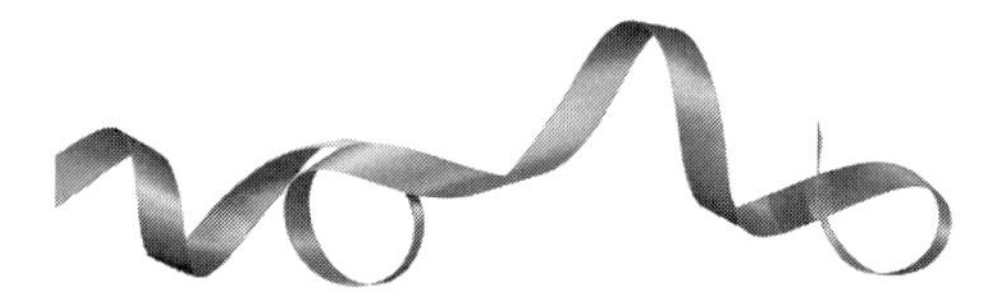

That night, I lay awake and breathed shallowly, my mind on high alert. I marveled at what my life had become.

Maybe an hour later, Leah tired of her knife-dancing. She casually dropped the knife on the stairs and climbed into bed. Her movements were like a zombie's, plodding and unconscious, and she didn't acknowledge my presence at all. I dozed once and woke to her snoring soundly. I was so tired. All I wanted to do was sleep, but that seemed unwise, maybe even dangerous. I climbed out of bed quietly and retrieved the knife where she had dropped it on the stairs. It felt like ice in my hands.

I knew I needed to call a doctor immediately. I walked downstairs and picked up the phone. No dial tone. I knelt down to check and make sure it was still plugged in. The cord had been cut. I rubbed my hands against the sharp edge. I walked across the living room and checked my cell. The cord was also cut, and my phone was dead. I went back to the hall to make sure she wasn't coming down and then surveyed the room to discover she had done this to everything: the computer, the coffee machine, the fridge. The cords were all plugged in their sockets but dangling limp. With the electronics disconnected, the house was quiet with a pall of death. Outside, the horizon was beginning to brighten. It was time for me to leave.

I went to the car and found the lights had been left on. I turned the engine, and it coughed a death rattle, letting me know the battery was dead. I smiled when I saw that. Leah had been mean before but never destructive. Now she had danced with a knife dangling over my head and cut me off from the outside world.

I went back inside and grabbed a coat and my dead phone to make the two-mile walk to Matt's. The chill in the air invigorated me. I no longer felt so bone tired. My breath came out in white clouds. The pines in the icy pre-dawn loomed tall and foreboding. They knew the secrets of this place. I wasn't so sure I wanted to anymore.

I stepped off the road several times to allow large logging trucks to whistle by me, each one a sure threat to suck me up and take me under. They rattled through the semi-darkness, driving as if being chased by spirits, red lights disappearing in the distance.

Besides the logging trucks, I was alone on the road. The day was gradually unfolding, but the shadows were still long, and I shivered in my light jacket. I was probably halfway there. Without the electric buzz that dulled my senses most of my waking moments, there was nothing to break the constant murmur in my head. What happened? Where had my wife gone? What was this madness that had so completely consumed her? My world had been swallowed up whole. My muscles ached, and my head was numb. I wanted to cry but didn't know if I had the tears. I wanted to blame the place, my own base desires, my wife for flicking me to the ground like a discarded cigarette, and Catherine for forgetting me when I needed her most.

Matt met me at the door with a cup of coffee in his hand. He knew this was not good.

"What happened?"

I felt like a traitor, turning on the one person I had promised everything to, but I said it anyway. "She's cracked. Fully cracked"

My wife, reduced to these awful words. I tried so hard not to cry. But there I was—crumpled in a ball in the driveway, crying desperate tears.

# CHAPTER 22

Meredith made a reservation for 9:30 p.m. and read for another forty-five minutes before getting ready. Michael showed her what he planned to wear—a well-made blue dress shirt and jeans. She grabbed them up and told him she'd put them in the wash. She knew the clothes would be ready well before she would. She retreated to her bathroom to take a long, hot bath.

Meredith liked her baths very hot—even uncomfortable at first. Lance had always complained about it and wouldn't join her, missing another chance at intimacy that would have regularly led to other things. She chuckled as she carefully put her foot in the tub, her skin turning pink in the heat. She eased herself in and waited for the level to be high enough to turn on the jets.

Then a strange thing happened: she noticed her body—she noticed her nakedness. Those things had gone without any real attention for so long, but now she saw them differently. She thought about the way her body ached and longed to be noticed by someone who would pay attention to her and let her lose herself. She closed her eyes, letting her hands explore, and marveled at how long it had been since she had done that. She tensed with the thought of the complications Michael brought. But sometimes complications were good …

The book was not just good; it was great. But what did Michael really have in store, and how exactly did she fit within his plan? He acted like he had enough money, but did he expect more? Did he want to stay here—with her? She wanted him to but had no idea how it would work. One thing was for certain: she wanted to end the night like she imagined Catherine would. She fantasized about what would come next when Catherine embraced the narrator and met his expectant kiss. She saw herself as Catherine, glad to be away from her brutish husband and into safe arms, healing the brokenness Leah had left him with, forgetting words and finding solace and bliss.

Slowly she nodded off. She dreamed of The Shoals and walking its grounds. She saw Catherine on the porch, waiting for her man. Catherine turned and noticed Meredith standing there. She shook her head and looked Meredith in the eyes. Just as Catherine started to speak, Meredith sensed another person there, a character she didn't know. She shook wide awake, startled.

Meredith looked around the room, panting. No one was there. Michael's footfalls sounded below. She glanced at her phone; thirty minutes had passed. She wanted to spend another half hour wallowing in her tub, but she had to get ready. She wanted to be with Michael. She wanted to know him. She wanted to untangle his secrets.

Michael was complicated. Despite the obstacles he faced, he had chosen to reveal himself to her, which made her feel special and sexy. He liked her, and the passion burned bright in his eyes, but she still didn't know enough about him. An extraordinary author, her idol, yet he might be a murderer as well. If she were being honest, she would admit his cloak of mystery turned her on.

Meredith leaped out of the tub, suddenly anxious to begin the night. She would put on her sexiest dress, dab perfume on the nape of her neck, and she would decipher this fascinating and enigmatic man.

They decided to go to The Olde Pink House, a Savannah

institution, for dinner. Meredith worried going out in public like this would be a problem, but he told her he did it all the time for short periods. His face had adorned enough book jackets that someone likely would comment on a resemblance if he stayed in one place for days, but he had government-issued IDs for his personas if he needed them, and he was used to shrugging and saying, "I get that a lot." Still, he always felt it best to be careful. He picked dark places and went later at night so people had already been drinking and were less likely to be thinking about missing literati.

She chose the restaurant because of its weekend crowds. It was the perfect meeting place for them to hide in plain sight. Meredith always felt uneasy walking around the building. She had once badly twisted her ankle in the restaurant due to the uneven surfaces between rooms and the servers constantly careening around corners with heavy trays of quail and seafood.

Then there were the ghosts; local lore claimed ghosts still roamed, even during the busiest hours. The son of the builder, a Revolutionary War hero named James Habersham, was said to visit with guests from time to time in the bar. She knew it would be right up Michael's alley.

A hundred pages from the end of the book, the one Meredith didn't want to stop reading, she now had a challenge: to see whether she could breathe life back into this once-great man just like he had done to her *Red Ribbon.* She still hadn't gotten in a rhythm with Michael, but she liked that he didn't force it. His face itself didn't tell many secrets, but the flash in his eyes did. They gave away blasts of raw emotion, a hint of what he would be like as a lover. The suspense of his entry combined with the romance of the book had eaten her up. She was with a man she had loved for twenty years.

# RED RIBBON

## CHAPTER EIGHTEEN

On the Saturday after Leah's latest commitment, when I was back at The Shoals with new cords and appliances and feeling as lonely as a country song, the weather turned warmer. It was almost Valentine's Day.

After Leah had been taken, I spent the night in Atlanta in another strip mall hotel. In my former life, I would have disdained the nondescript rooms; now, it felt safe and normal.

I fantasized about buying a one-way ticket to the Caribbean, Greece, or anywhere but The Shoals. But I couldn't leave her now. The doctors needed me, and she needed me, and frankly, being alone at The Shoals didn't feel much different than being with her.

Weeks passed with generic phone calls that only highlighted the distance between us. I pondered new work. I dutifully kept working on the project, hoping I would find more treasures. I awaited the moment when the air would start to warm, and I would surely renew my digging outside. I knew the one thing I needed more than anything else was to search through the dirt. Now that Catherine didn't visit anymore, it was the one thing I looked forward to.

I found a spot halfway down to the river where I could still see the house but was a little further out. Maybe there I would turn up something new.

After a few false starts, I finally got a rhythm. By then, the sun was high enough to make it reasonable to shed the jacket. The thin sunlight hinted at spring. I felt alive for the first time since being in Catherine's arms.

I sat down to rest for a minute. This was Leah's family's land. Sure it had been paid for with my money, but it had been in her family for six generations. I needed to consider how much longer I would be welcome at The Shoals and how much longer I would want to stay.

It had been almost four months since I last saw Catherine, yet she was somehow never far. The feel of her skin, the way her head rested on my shoulder, the hope in her voice. When Leah was away, I still looked for her, still turned my head for footsteps that might be coming down the road, and awaited a soft knocking at the door. I couldn't bear to think she might only be a memory.

I watched a hawk fly across the land below, not aware of the problems we humans had. He soared and circled, defying the law of gravity. He glided with ease and purpose, and when he spotted his prey, he drew a straight line through the air and caught the field mouse in a single movement.

I went back to my hunt. I imagined that hawk and tried to channel the grace of his purpose and tried to stay out of my head.

After a while, the detector made a different sound than I had heard it make before. I didn't have a way of determining what type of metal I had ahead of me, but by the finder, I could tell it wasn't far under. I put my shovel in the ground, and I was away on my next adventure.

That was my first truly major find: an ornate metal pouch with initials I couldn't read. I brushed away the dirt, but I would have to wash it at home to read it clearly. It was very old and hadn't been disturbed in many years. I placed it gently on a rock and picked up the detector again. I was about to continue, to see what else the land held when, just like that hawk, I spied someone far away, moving toward my house. A woman. When she got there, she sat down on the front steps. My stomach dropped in a panic. Was Leah home? Then the breeze picked up her hair, and I saw a flash of red—her familiar ribbon. It was Catherine, returning to me! I left my belongings where they were and raced down the steep hill. Catherine! Oh Catherine!

# Chapter 23

The walk to the restaurant took less than ten minutes, another advantage of living in small-town Savannah.

"I love the feel of the old southern cities. They've got a permanence to them so many other places don't," Michael said.

"Is that why you chose Charleston?" This was the first time he had talked in this way, and Meredith hung on every word.

"I never really wrote about my growing up, but I was born there. I traveled a little, but my family owned an insurance business, and it made sense for me to come back."

He continued opening up as they strolled down the street. "I didn't belong behind a desk. I was maybe the worst insurance agent in history. But it gave me time to slip away and start writing."

The slick paver stones glistened after the day's rain, and as a streetlight caught his face, Meredith noticed just how handsome he was. His clothes looked much better after the wash, and he seemed more in his element now that he wasn't so bedraggled. He walked straighter and even held out his arm for her as they got near the entrance.

He smiled brightly as they approached the hostess. She told them it would be several minutes before their table was ready, so they headed for the basement bar and ordered drinks. He put his hand gently on hers.

His half-grin drove her crazy; Michael could be rakishly charming when he wanted to.

When the drinks arrived, Michael's eyes lit up as he looked at Meredith. She smiled like he was putting a ring on her finger.

He lifted his glass, and she mirrored him.

"To tonight and a thousand more just like it." His eyes tore through her.

She touched her glass to his.

When she finished her first glass of Merlot, she forgot about worrying about his fugitive status and let herself sink into the moment and enjoy being with him.

It wouldn't take much to get her drunk—and she was quite okay with that.

Meredith replayed the toast. She shook her head and paused, turning straight to Michael. "Why are you being so generous?"

He looked down at his glass and then up at her. "I've told you."

She shook her head again. "Come on. There's more."

"You want the truth?"

"Nothing but." Their shoulders touched, and she turned her body away so she could hear his answer.

He smiled as she rested her hand on his knee. He turned and did the same on her leg, a little higher.

"Truth is I'm lonely and I'm bored. I needed something to do, and I want someone to do it with. I have thought many times about not being Michael Black and creating a new backstory, pretending all of this"—he swept his hand around the room as if he owned it—"never happened. But I can't do that. I'm Michael Black. I'm a writer. It's not something I can give up easily."

"Pick a pen name and write under that. Plenty of authors write anonymously."

Michael shook his head vigorously. "No, it wouldn't work. I can't re-enter the publishing world. Quinn's old man really has it out for me. He never believed I died, and if he so much as sensed I was back writing—either under my name or a pen name—he has enough money and connections to put me away for forever."

"But isn't *Red Ribbon* exactly that? Your new novel written under a pen name?"

"Yeah, but you have a great cover story. You can show you sent me the manuscript years ago. You can say I gave you great editorial advice and the success of the store re-energized you and inspired you to start writing again. I specifically chose different ways of phrasing and structuring things so it wouldn't read exactly like a Michael Black novel. It's your story with my writing, but it's got a different feel."

The second glass of wine, combined with the endearing words from Michael, made her blush the color of the Merlot. Thinking about it only made it worse. "You've really thought this through." She looked at her wine glass and then him.

He smiled and gazed straight into her eyes. "I've planned everything."

Meredith reached over and kissed him on the cheek. "I—"

Michael laughed and shook her off. "Well that was a nice surprise."

"You're making my dreams come true." She didn't mean to give away so much, but she couldn't help it. He amazed her and flustered her. She would have to keep it to herself and trust no one with her secret, but it was still unreal. And such a good book.

Across the room, the piano player played the Savannah classic, Johnny Mercer's "Moon River." The music transported Meredith to a different time, when the classics were created. She looked at Michael. She saw a man who had chosen her for all the reasons a woman would want to be chosen—for her body *and* her mind. She moved a little closer to him. He didn't hesitate and slipped in to give her a quick kiss on the lips, a lover's kiss, one that danced and ended too soon.

The hostess stood behind them, unfazed by their display. Michael looked at Meredith in a way that left no doubt where the night would lead.

"To dinner and a show," he said.

It only took a moment for Meredith to understand exactly what he meant.

# RED RIBBON

## CHAPTER NINETEEN

I don't remember the sprint that brought me down that hill. I remember getting close enough to lock eyes and know what we both needed. Her lips tasted salty, and I devoured them. Her body pressed to mine, and I felt her breasts against my chest. I wrapped my arm around the small of her back.

The kiss seemed to last a lifetime. The world stopped spinning around us. The birds stopped their song in silent anticipation. I moved down to kiss her neck, nibbling at her warm, soft skin. When I bit harder, her breath left her, and she relaxed into my arms.

I pulled back and looked at her, my hands cupping her face. She was even more beautiful than I remembered. Her eyes were soft and inquisitive, and her body curved gently. When our eyes met, I finally understood her relationship with her husband. Those scars were from him; he hurt her. I pulled her against me, trying to protect her with my arms. Then I took her by the hand and lead her into the house.

We blew through the door.

My heart seized when I saw Leah sitting there.

# CHAPTER 24

The hostess sat them upstairs in a small room, winking at Meredith as she handed them their menus. Meredith smiled brightly, and Michael met her eyes and reached for her hand. She felt like she was in one of Michael's books—the glamorous opening when the characters were just starting to let down their guards. And Michael seemed to be matching her interest. The mood—and the wine—wiped away any hard-hitting questions Meredith might have intended to ask. Instead, she turned to the book. Her book.

After they ordered some food and more wine, Meredith asked, "If I decided I wanted to publish, what would happen next?"

Michael slowly broke into a grin. "If?"

Meredith lowered her eyes and chuckled at her embarrassment. "Fine. When I decide to."

"We will get you a publishing deal and set a publication date."

She shook her head, remembering the constant rejections. "It will happen that easily?"

Michael closed his eyes and nodded.

What seemed like a herculean task for her, clearly didn't bother him. "How long will it take to come out?"

"We're headed into the fourth quarter, and no one wants to publish a new author against all the heavyweights. My guess would be just over a year from now."

Meredith slumped a little. She wanted the process to take less time.

"Books are like ocean liners," he said. "They take time to build momentum, and they're hard to turn around. Don't worry. The time will move quickly."

"Can I say yes now?"

He chuckled. "You said yes as soon as you started reading."

She squeezed his hand. "Am I that easy to read?"

He shook his head lightly. "I just happen to be rather good at it."

The three glasses of Merlot and lack of food were going to be doing much of the talking from here on out. She could sense it. "What else are you good at?"

Before he could answer, the waiter brought their food. They giggled as their meals were revealed, her salmon, his bloody steak. They didn't speak for a moment, and then Michael cut a small piece of meat and put it on his fork for her. She looked in his eyes as she bit the meat off his fork. Her chest felt warm, and her legs were weak. Michael stared at her with an intensity so raw she had to stop herself from dragging him to the bathroom. She tasted and savored the tender meat. She nodded at him.

"How's your fish?"

"Delicious. Here." She cut a small piece and leaned over the table towards him.

His eyes fixed on her. He waited for her to put the bite in his mouth.

She found it strange he didn't blink as if he were engaged in a staring contest. She turned away, pretending it didn't bother her.

# Red Ribbon

## Chapter Twenty

Leah sat on the sofa inside, with eyes that reminded me of all the special words I had said to her in a seemingly different life. She looked like her old self, with color in her cheeks and a glint in her eyes. That hint of a comeback made it all that much worse—a betrayal on both sides, a man caught between two jilted women.

I froze. I came up with a thousand different things to say. None of them would come out of my mouth. Leah stood up, her eyes filled with passion, and walked straight toward me. She spoke no words. She stood right in front of me and kissed me like it was our wedding day. I wanted to join her there, but I was standing next to the woman I loved—in one of the most awkward moments of my life.

She finally pushed away. "Hey!" she said playfully. "Aren't you going to kiss me back?"

Leah play-pouted, finally adding, "Okay, maybe that was a little strong for all we've been through, but I'm back, and there's no way I'm letting this moment go without dragging you upstairs." She toyed with my shirt and brought her look back up to me. "I've been a bad girl, and I need to tell you all about it."

I worked up the courage to turn and look at my sweet Catherine, hoping she could give me the strength to tell Leah I didn't love her anymore. But Catherine was nowhere to be seen. The front door was open, and the midday light spilled in. I turned back to Leah. She was ready for another kiss.

"I'm so happy to see you! They said I could come home!"

Her energy was so real, so positive. I glimpsed the woman I had married. She wanted to kiss again, and I still had the rush of energy Catherine's reappearance had brought. Leah's electricity became contagious, but I realized halfway through a longer and even more substantial kiss that in my mind I was kissing my mistress and not my wife. She felt my erection and reached down to undo my jeans.

"I see you've been waiting for this too." She kissed me hungrily.

We didn't make it upstairs. I had the strangest moment of déjà vu—I was making love to the past and present at the same time, and I couldn't tell who was who. If Catherine were outside watching, as I was afraid she was, how could she ever forgive me? I told myself I couldn't worry, but I did. I tried my best to keep my mind focused by cheating with my wife.

# CHAPTER 25

The rain disappeared for the moment, and she carried her shawl. Michael extended his hand, and she took it gratefully.

"Now what?" Meredith pulled herself closer to him.

"I thought you could show me around a little bit. We spent way too much time at dinner talking about me. I have better manners than that. I want to know all about you."

She didn't answer for a second.

They strolled away from the river and through the heart of the market. Their walking developed a rhythm over the rough cobblestones.

She squeezed his hand.

He prompted her again. "Meredith?"

She sighed. "Oh, you know. Living out part of my dream with the bookstore but, at the same time, trying to get my feet back under me after my divorce. Sometimes, it feels like the loss from it is greater than anything I can accomplish; other times, I feel like I own the world—or at least Savannah. I always wanted to write about the contradictions women live with—how all the *you go, girl* stuff coexists with the sad and twisted things we're taught about ourselves and how we believe it."

"You should write about it."

Meredith heard the hint of boredom in his voice.

"I'm hoping this whole experience will let you open yourself to being a more creative being."

Occasionally, the trees dripped a leftover raindrop on the back of her neck. The clouds parted, and she could see the moon break through—the final piece of a perfect dream.

He seemed to read her mind and used her hand to turn her toward him like an experienced dancer leading his partner. His face lit by the moonlight, she could see the need in his eyes, and she knew he recognized the same in hers. He took his right hand and cradled her cheek, leaned in, and kissed her. She put her hand on his chest and wrapped her other arm around his waist. It was a tender kiss, different than the one at the bar, one that had been evolving over the decades. She drew back to see what he was thinking. His eyes were still closed. She wanted to reach up again, feel his lips on hers again, but he smiled and took her hand, and they continued walking.

Suddenly, Michael stopped her. "I was really interested in your library. I didn't get to look around much. Could you give me a guided tour?"—a line from his book *Cecelia*, which led to a sexy scene between the two main characters. He let a grin catch the corner of his mouth.

Meredith returned a knowing smile. "I thought you'd never ask, Mr. Havens." She squeezed his hand, sure she just passed yet another test, and the two walked back to her place.

# RED RIBBON

## Chapter Twenty-One

We fell asleep in a lovers' embrace after that surprising and poignant afternoon. It awoke feelings in me I was sure the winter had crushed. Maybe there was a chance. Maybe my wife had returned. We had met each other's energy and desire, and then we landed exhausted in each other's arms.

When I awoke, I gently moved my arm from underneath Leah's head. She was still asleep, her face serene. I was reluctant to look out the window, not knowing how to fix it, not wanting to short-change Leah even though she had often done that to me. I hoped for a return to normal. I hoped she would be gone for the moment and allow me my dream, but Catherine stood outside, staring up at my window. There were tears streaming down her face. Where I expected anger, there was only sadness.

I quietly ran downstairs. I had to explain. I was done with Leah. I had lost control, succumbed to habit.

By the time I reached the porch, she was gone, running down the road. For fear of waking Leah, I didn't call to her; instead I watched my lover go, the red ribbon bouncing in her hair.

It felt like hours that I sat frozen in that spot on the porch, the sun gently setting, illuminating the yard in yellows and oranges. The light reminded me of our first day walking the place. My heart broke for the millionth time since I had arrived. When Catherine left, I heard something I had never heard before—a low, constant moaning noise. Perhaps it was there before, but I never noticed it. Now, the low and steady cries were all I heard. The temperature dropped, but I didn't move, transfixed by the sorrowful sound. I betrayed two women yet again that day. I heard her crying for hours that night, long after I came in the house and shut the natural world out. Even after I returned to bed, the moonlight grazing Leah's shoulder as she slept, I could still hear it. It seemed to get louder the closer I was to my wife.

# Chapter 26

They made it back to her house, somehow still fully clothed.

Inside, as soon as the door closed, they met again. Meredith pulled him to her and lost herself in the kissing. His breath felt hot on her neck, her breasts, her back. Michael unzipped her dress and in one motion undid the clasp of her bra. She made small, yearning sounds as he kissed her again. Then he turned his attention to her neck. She focused as much as possible, trying to enjoy every sliver of this dreamy night. Instead of thinking about what she wished he was doing, as she would have with Lance, she concentrated on how incredible she felt and savored this perfect moment: the way his teeth nibbled her neck, the way his hair brushed across her cheek, the roughness of his hands on her breasts. This man sensed her longing and matched her feelings. He could deftly and confidently make love to her the way she had known only through the pages of books.

She tore at his shirt with a surprising violence, sending buttons flying across the floor. He took her hands and pushed her against the wall, held on, and then kissed her in that spot, biting her lip harder and harder until she moved her head back and came back at him.

She wrenched her hands away and put her palms on his chest. “Take me upstairs—now.”

He kissed her again at the top of the stairs, his hand reaching down and touching between her legs. She didn't resist. She merely met his eyes and motioned to the room just ahead. He pushed her onto the bed and began to push her dress above her. He kissed her again, hard, and took a second to look at her. Under his gaze, Meredith felt beautiful, sexy, and complete. Yet never before had a man's look so completely disarmed her. She took his hand and moved it to her breast, her nipple tingling through the fabric of her dress. The way he touched her assured her she didn't need to worry about him. He was her hero, and he was about to become her lover.

"Can I suggest something you may find odd?" he asked.

She nodded, although she didn't want to.

He started taking off his clothes, and after a beat, she did the same. He climbed onto the bed and crossed his legs into a lotus position.

"Here, sit on top of me like this." He moved her so her legs sat on top of his. "Come here close." He maneuvered them so their foreheads touched. He took her hand and placed it on his chest, on top of where his heart lay. Then he placed his palm in the same place on her, over her heart. "This is a third eye kiss. It connects us—our heads, our hearts, and our bodies."

She looked deep into his eyes, her breathing slowing to match his, her body calming with every deep breath. This felt so much more intimate than sex. She noticed the way her entire body began to feel the difference. She still longed for his body, but she felt the exercise left other parts of her open. She could imagine a deeper relationship with this man—one she desperately wanted.

"We're exchanging energy. It's a powerful thing. It's not something—"

She cut him off. "I want you to take me," she said. "I can't wait any longer."

"Completely?"

"Completely."

He eased her off of him and laid her gently on the bed. The moonlight from the window rested softly on her cheeks.

She wanted the moment to extend forever.

He inched down the bed until his head was between her legs. He looked up at her, and their eyes met.

Then she grasped for the sheets.

He had her.

Completely.

# RED RIBBON

## CHAPTER TWENTY-FIVE

Oh God. Not again.

Just as I had gotten used to Leah being back—not quite insane but still sucking my joy away moment by moment—and as I lay so close to drifting off in dreams, I heard her. Outside. Yelling.

I wearily rose and walked to the door. I rubbed my eyes and opened them. There, down the path, silhouetted by the moon, I saw Leah.

"I have her!" She screamed at me.

"What are you talking about?" I yelled back. It felt odd even though no one was around.

"Your homewrecker!"

I wanted to scream at her, tell her she was the one who had wrecked our home, but like so many other times, I kept quiet.

"What are you talking about?"

"Your little whore. Catherine I guess is her name."

I wanted to cut out her tongue for breathing my Catherine's sacred name. I threw on a pair of pajama pants and the flip-flops I kept by the door. I was thankful for the moonlight as it made it easier to navigate in the night. The crickets and the frogs were unperturbed and filled the air with nighttime sounds.

I started moving toward her. I couldn't see Catherine but couldn't take a chance.

"Leah? What's wrong, honey?"

"Don't try to lie to me anymore. She comes into my head and tells me what you're doing."

Was that true? It couldn't be. I felt sick.

Leah was enjoying my attention, which I have to admit I regularly withheld. She was ahead of me, half-running, half-dancing, leading me down the hill, away from the house and into what now seemed like her domain.

The moonlight was bright and summer was approaching. I noticed how the light seemed to lay on top of the trees. Had she done something to Catherine? Oh please, God, no.

"Leah? This makes no sense."

"And you aren't responding to my accusations!" she said as she danced on ahead. Her voice seemed eerie and free. She was beginning to unnerve me.

She moved behind an old tree, big enough to hide her small body completely behind it. She didn't reappear.

"Come … here!" she said.

I still couldn't see her. "Leah? This is madness. Is everything okay?"

"Come … here."

I walked down the path cautiously, searching through the trees for where she might have gone. "Leah?"

I heard the step from behind a moment too late. I turned to face her when I felt a blow to the back of my head. I hit the ground and was out cold.

# CHAPTER 27

At 7:30 the next morning, she awoke, her head on his chest, light flooding through the window. Meredith decided not to play coy. She kissed his neck and put her hands between his legs. She toyed with him, slowly at first, and then looked up at him.

"I'm older than you, you know." He grinned.

"Well, I can stop any time. Just let me know."

"Don't stop," he said as he closed his eyes.

She played with him for several minutes until he turned the tables and buried his head beneath the sheets.

"I'm not used to this much attention."

"Lance didn't know how to do this?"

"I really don't want to think about Lance right now." She pushed his head down harder.

* * *

Michael went back to sleep, but Meredith felt restless. Wide awake, she practically pranced through the bedroom totally nude, something she never did. She felt warm inside and out. She wanted him to join her, maybe have an early breakfast or go for a walk down River Street holding hands. Then reality hit again. She wanted to show him off, bring him everywhere with her, but she knew she had to keep him a secret.

She finally returned to bed, cuddling against him while he dozed. Finally, she couldn't wait any longer. "What are you thinking about?"

"Did you finish the book?"

She shook her head. "I told you I didn't. Don't you remember?"

"I was preoccupied with other things last night."

"I almost forgot how badly I wanted to read it—if you're done treating me with sexual favors, that is."

"Enjoy it. Get back to it," he said. "Maybe I'll take a long bath in the tub I saw in there—if it's okay with you, of course." He motioned to the master bath.

Meredith smiled so wide it felt like her face might break. "Sounds great."

Michael walked naked to the bathroom.

When she heard the water start running, she grabbed the manuscript on the bedside table and headed back to the story.

# RED RIBBON

## CHAPTER TWENTY-SEVEN

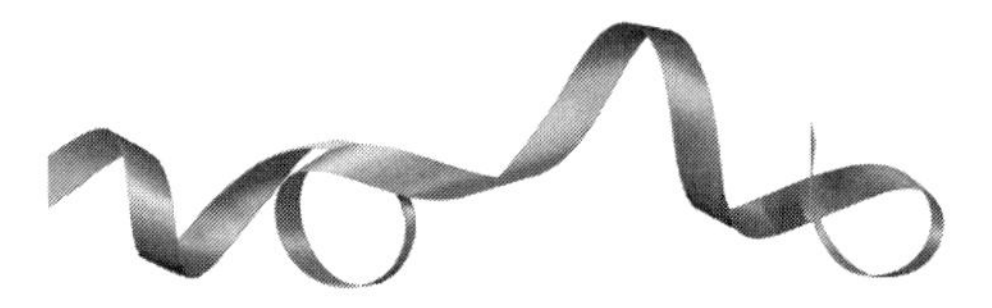

When I awoke, Leah stood over me like Florence Nightingale. Matt and Penelope were there as well.

Matt smiled. He was trying too hard. I wondered what she had told them. "That'll teach you not to go out in the middle of the night with damn flip flops on."

I hadn't seen Matt for months. What was this all about? My mind was molasses, but I remembered it slowly. The accusations. The chase. Now why was Leah smiling and cooing and acting like I was the one who needed help?

I wanted to say something but held back. I didn't know Matt well enough to tell him this crazy story. I was learning I didn't know any of these people. What had Leah done with Catherine?

"Catherine," I said, not caring who heard.

"Who's Catherine?" Penelope asked, perplexed.

"He means me." Leah beamed. "My middle name is Catherine."

Of course, it wasn't.

I glared a hole right through her.

She stared at me, not giving an inch. "Now let me give you some medicine," she said softly. "You need to go back to sleep."

My head pounded. I knew I shouldn't take it, but I did. And it put me out immediately.

# Chapter 28

She had nearly finished the book. Michael could wait a while longer. She needed to question herself, make sure her motives were right for following through with this.

Meredith had a great life. She had a great house. She enjoyed her job. She made good money. Hell, she attracted her very own hero into her bed.

Was it crazy to throw it all away for *Red Ribbon*?

Maybe.

The rational part of her brain reminded her of the creepy way Michael came into her life. What people said about him and his relationships. What he would likely be charged with if he reemerged. She tried to recreate the moment she saw her own number on the caller ID.

But every time those concerns settled in her mind, her yearning to be a writer drowned them out. She thought of the hours and days and months she spent dreaming of what she held in her hands. She thought of last night and the space they shared. The tender way he held her body, the feel of his tongue on her most intimate spaces. The way she felt this morning, alive on every level. Powerful, sexy, smart.

If Meredith had wanted to play it safe, she never should have read the book. She knew what she was doing, and she knew what she wanted. Her thighs quivered with thoughts of last night's loving. She felt alive again.

# RED RIBBON

## CHAPTER TWENTY-NINE

The first couple of days, I took the pills. By the way I felt afterwards, I assumed they were heavy sedatives, but I didn't mind the constant sleep, and I needed the rest. I didn't know exactly what had happened in the woods, but I knew enough to know I couldn't lay down forever.

On the fourth day, when she had begun to assume I didn't understand her role in all of this, I tucked the pill under my tongue, and when she left, I flushed it down the toilet. That afternoon, I almost wished I hadn't as the pain from the back of my head came back. But I was thankful for the ability to think again.

It was another vibrant summer night, laced with the smells and sounds of the Georgia forest, when I saw her again on the lawn as the sun began to set. She laid out candles on the ground in a circle, talking to herself.

She arranged the candles systematically, lighting them after the last preparations were made. She looked back toward the house once, and I wondered if there was someone else around, maybe the person who had put the gash in my head. I stood by the window, trying to hide and still see what was going on.

I needed to get closer. I needed to hear what she was saying.

Before I had a chance to put on my shoes, I saw her blow out the candles and head back for the house. Had I spooked her? I quickly jumped back in bed and clamped my eyes shut, hoping she wouldn't notice.

I could hear her. She made small noises, repetitive clicks and trills that made me think she was talking backwards. The sounds scraped against my skull and filled my whole body with dread.

I still had my eyes closed when I sensed she was back in the room. I could only imagine what it would be this time. She waved something over my face, and I didn't move. She did it one more time for good measure. When she was satisfied I wasn't going to wake, she whispered. It was not my wife's voice, and yet it was.

"Two more days. Then they'll be here. Two more days."

She noticed I wasn't stirring, so she said it again. Just a little louder, gloating this time. "Two more days."

# Chapter 29

Michael sat in the tub. He had found a Raymond Chandler novel in a corner of Meredith's library. He noticed it the first time he made one of his visits into her home, but now he could spend some time with it. He had read it half a dozen times, but in each read, he found something new. *The Long Goodbye* was about as good of a book as you could find in his estimation. He wondered if she had picked it up after the piece he had written about it for *Harper's* many years ago. Of course, she was more well-read than most, so he couldn't guarantee it, but it seemed like a good bet to him.

He wondered when she would finish *Red Ribbon*. Would she immediately make the connection? He figured she would; she was a smart cookie. She was a worthy inclusion into his life. He hoped she would understand just how much he was going to mean to her. She would have to let him come and go and let him surprise her from time to time. His current status meant he couldn't be tied down in any traditional way, and he hoped she could see the freedom that meant for her. She didn't need to know just yet about how all this tied together; he had the plan, and for it to work, he would have to explain it as time went on.

Michael sunk down deeper in the hot water. At least he passed the first test. He enjoyed the night before, and the passion had been better than he expected. He knew it had something to do with her intelligence and probably, as much as it hurt him to say it, with her maturity. As shiny as Quinn was, she could not have had the same experience Meredith had.

Of course, there had been others in between, but he never allowed himself to connect beyond the carnal. He indulged regularly, always when he visited a big city, always when he loaded the debit card and set himself up for a couple nights at a hotel. Originally, he would try to use the liaisons as a place to stay, but those situations led him into his stalking routine, which he found distasteful and a waste of time spent on those beneath him. Invariably, if he knew where they lived, curiosity would get the better of him, and he would wind up spending weeks on a woman who wasn't worthy.

He developed his rules, and to his credit, he stuck to them. But living life at that level of interaction led him to start the full-on press with Meredith. Unlike the others, impressing her meant something. If all went according to plan, he could write the story he wanted with the companion who had eluded him for years.

It could all go wrong in the next few minutes. If she saw too much in what he had written or if she figured out the key he had hidden, it could be over—or even worse, she could turn him in. He had planned his escape route just in case. While he waited, he re-read Chandler's classic. There were many worse ways to spend a tense moment.

# RED RIBBON

## CHAPTER THIRTY

I waited until I knew she was well out of the room, and then I waited a little longer. When I opened my eyes, I saw she had almost closed the door. I looked outside and saw Catherine looking at me through the window. She looked at me with a mix of love and fear. I motioned her to stay quiet and threw on a pair of tennis shoes.

I walked softly to the door, holding my breath and praying it didn't creak.

Outside, her eyes met mine. "You've got to go. I've tried to get to you and warn you," Catherine whispered.

"I get it. I'm leaving now."

She reached to my lips and kissed me softly. "One thing. Please make sure she's not hurt."

My eyes widened. That was not what I was expecting.

"She's not one of them or, at least, not yet," she said. "She doesn't know it was not his fault." She looked at me earnestly. "Don't doom her."

Maybe my look gave me away. I was so confused, but suddenly, a feeling came over me. An understanding. A dread and a fascinating calm. A shock beyond any revelation I had ever experienced. I tried to make sure I understood. I wondered if this would be the last time I saw her, if knowledge of this strangeness would take her away from me.

I looked at her. "Did they take you the other night? Did they hurt you?"

The look she gave me was full of pity as if I didn't understand any of this.

"You can't hurt a ghost."

That word.

I understood. The scars. The strange manner of speaking. Her concern about this house. Her strange statements about the views. Of course you could see the river a hundred fifty years ago.

But her tortured eyes revealed that her words weren't true, that she was again trying to keep me safe as if her pain didn't matter. I closed my eyes for the briefest moment, trying to process all of this. When I looked back, wanting desperately to kiss her again, she was gone.

Then Leah started screaming.

# CHAPTER 30

Michael felt restless. He knew it would take her a reasonable time to finish the book, but he genuinely wanted to hear what she thought. He wasn't used to being in houses this long anymore. He knew he couldn't return to her carriage house, his hiding place of the last six weeks.

*Excuse me, Meredith. I'd like to go back to hiding in the corner where you clearly should have seen me every time you pulled into your garage.*

That would be strange—even to him.

*Excuse me. Are you aware every time you leave, I go in and rummage through your panty drawer and sniff every bit of your dirty laundry? I picked this week because you're about to go on your period, and I knew you would be extra sexual and emotional?*

There were no dowagers hiding him out in Europe. He had never left the states, figuring he would get caught going through international security. His identities had been established long before Quinn became so clingy and unrealistic. He wasn't going to marry her, but she wouldn't shut up about it. She grew angrier and angrier, and when she came home with a pregnancy test, well, he couldn't take it. He knew he might eventually need good papers. His friends all told him she was too young and didn't understand how the world worked. But he would smile and think of her ass shining in the air. He told them a twenty-two-year-old girl was like puppy's breath. There just wasn't anything better.

But oh, she was an idiot, and he couldn't stand her hanging around anymore, nagging him. She had planned to trap him, but he had more brains. He lured her out by asking her to go on a drive with him so they could *talk*, and he did what he had to. The escape was easy. He paid a fortune to spend three months on a Montana ranch, letting his hair grow long, wearing sunglasses, and camping. He did miss one thing though: being recognized as the master he was. He missed being Michael Black. He missed the publicity, the book signings, and the awards banquets. He missed getting blowjobs from suburban housewives in bookstore bathrooms.

He had hidden money in five different places—some investments hidden in shells and some accounts. The investments had proven to be winners. Thank God he had also opened up a bank account in the name of one of his characters before regulations nearly made it impossible to open up new accounts without ten different photo IDs and seventeen credit cards. He had nursed the relationship at the small bank in south Texas to the point everyone—caretaker to president—knew him as Jim Andrews. He could go there any time without fear of being found out.

He communicated with his confidants once a year and let them know he was okay. He did this cryptically, of course, but it worked just the same.

After six months on the lam, he fell out of national memory. Writers, other than maybe Mr. King and Ms. Rowling, have a short shelf life. They didn't warrant exposure on TV. If they wanted to drop off the scene and disappear, so be it. Even if they had a crazy family trailing them, thinking they had killed a woman.

The isolation made him itch and his skin burn. Then six months ago he read the article about Meredith's store and came up with the plan to bring her back in his life. He admitted to himself he had moved further and further from social norms, although his behavior back when she first wrote him was weird enough; he was just much better at letting it go unnoticed.

# RED RIBBON

## Chapter Thirty-One

I walked inside and could hear Leah above. Her voice spewed anger and confusion.

"It's not what you think," I said, wanting to calm the situation down.

"What I think? I think I have an unfaithful husband who also conspires with the general!"

I sighed deeply. "The general?"

"You know what I mean."

I still couldn't see her. It sounded like she was rummaging around for something. I certainly wasn't going to rush up there until I knew what I was facing. "Leah?"

The dead silence chilled me.

"Leah?"

I heard her walk closer to the downstairs. The floorboards still creaked as she approached.

"Leah?"

The creaks headed in my direction. She breathed audibly but no answer.

Step.

Creak.

"What's wrong?"

Step.

Creak.

She finally spoke. "You violated our wedding bed."

Step.

Creak.

"With a woman of a scarlet reputation"

Step.

Creak.

"You created this," she said, with death in a voice that seemed to be coming from someone else.

Step.

Creak.

I could see her now. Her eyes were black and unknowable. She scowled and nearly spit the hatred at me. She held the same knife she had danced with in her hand. She held it differently, more expertly. She took each step slowly and deliberately.

"What do you say to these charges?"

I didn't know what to say. I didn't know what to do. I was foolishly standing at the landing, but I didn't move when she made her move, jumping the final half-dozen steps in the hopes of knifing me then and there.

I had enough presence of mind to move slightly and focus on the knife. I was able to fend off the main blow, but it still cut my finger deeply, and I began to bleed. I could hear her banshee screams, and the knife skid away to the corner. She leaped toward it, and I tried to follow.

It was something about the blood. As I felt the sting of the cut and saw my blood—how dare she shed my blood!—my calm left me. My reason left me. This woman had robbed me of my hope, then let me believe a sliver of it was returning, only to bring me down yet again. She raced toward the knife, but she was no match for me. I ran after her and pushed her to the ground. I saw everything. And I was enraged. I grabbed the knife and stabbed her—again and again. I welcomed her cries. I welcomed her blood. It was going to end like this—her or me.

And after a year of sacrificing my life for hers, I had had enough.

"No more," I said.

She struggled, and I heard the wet attempt at breath. I could feel the blood under us and rolled off of her. The knife stuck out of her ribcage. It was in deep. I couldn't pull it out.

And then it was gone. My rage was gone, and regret smothered me completely. She coughed and wheezed loudly, struggling for life. She looked at me with horror and tried to speak, but I put a finger to her lips. I think she was Leah then. My Leah. I think I was back to being me, and I wanted to throw up. 9-1-1 wouldn't save her. She was going to die unless her ghosts could save her. I knew they couldn't; they couldn't save themselves. I looked at her tenderly, thinking about my beautiful wife. My bride and joy. I couldn't imagine her pain being any greater than mine.

I kneeled by her. "Do you need anything?"

She shook her head. She knew.

# Chapter 31

Despite his ability to write about normal men and women, he was clearly not one of them. His ideal relationship amounted to a bookstore blowjob. All the release, excitement, fear of being caught, none of the having to listen to her later.

About a month and a half ago, he went to Meredith's store every day for a week, even buying a couple of books. He didn't worry about anyone noticing him; he looked radically different than he had in his previous life. He knew the address of her house, and he came by daily, just on a stroll, knowing it would eventually lead to more. He bribed a shady locksmith and had a key made. Then he moved into her carriage house. It was big enough for what he needed, and he had enough experience watching people to know how to quietly take up space in a way they wouldn't notice. Meredith's place had been easy; her space was detached, and she never kept the light on. It felt nearly like a regular house after he feathered his nest.

He loved getting close enough to feel the women he stalked—see them, smell them, taste them—all without them knowing he did so. It was a different type of intrusion, a different type of joining of two lives. He didn't have to tell them anything. He achieved intimacy without having to share it.

He actually preferred a dank post to being inside her house. He felt exhausted from having to constantly put on a show.

Michael wondered if something was wrong. Meredith was taking an excruciatingly long time. Maybe she wasn't even there. Maybe she had run to the police and told them the murderer of Quinn Yancey stayed at her house. Maybe he should look out the window and see if they were there.

He tried to refocus on the book. But his eyes slid off the page. Quinn could speak to Meredith through the manuscript. She was planning for his trial. He could feel those cold chains on his wrists as they walked him down the hallway to death row, the prison uniform sagging on his body.

Then Meredith walked in.

The water felt lukewarm, and he'd been in the tub so long his whole body had turned into a prune. She didn't seem to notice; her eyes wouldn't focus on him. She sat down on the floor beside the tub and finally looked at him.

"Is The Shoals a real place?"

He nodded. "It's closer to Augusta than Atlanta."

"So you changed that. Why?"

He shrugged. "Great little details about the general. Worth putting in."

She bit her lip.

He could tell she wanted to be diplomatic, and he promised himself to play it cool, even though his heart pounded in his chest.

"If I go there, say tomorrow, am I going to find any …"

"Surprises?" he laughed.

"Surprises. That's a good word." She watched him intently.

He could do this. "Darling, if we get in the car and drive up to The Shoals, you won't find anything buried there. I just felt it needed some real detail to bring everything together."

She looked skeptical. "Then why use a real place?"

Michael had practiced this next expression. It needed to appear mirthful. It helped that, as ridiculous as it was, it was also true. "I know the guy who owns the place. He's an asshole. I want him to have to deal with all the crowds." He gave her his best Cheshire cat grin.

She laughed. She needed this to work.

They both knew she couldn't let this opportunity go.

She looked at her watch. A good portion of Saturday had already slipped away, and Georgia would be kicking off soon at 3 p.m. "Want to watch some football with me, then ravage me again, and then plan for a road trip?"

Michael smiled like a benevolent king, the pieces of his plan falling into place. "Go Dawgs," he said, "as much as it pains a South Carolinian to say so."

# Red Ribbon

## Chapter Thirty-Two

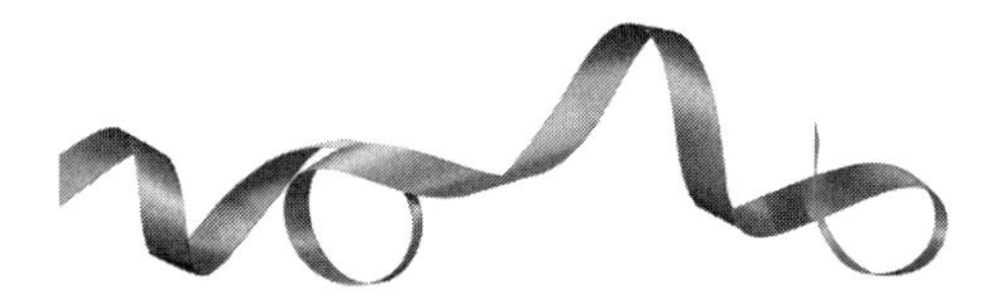

Oh, dear, God. What did I do? What terrible, soul-killing thing had I done? Everything was covered in blood, and her body had gone limp and heavy. I laid her body down in the hall and set off in search of matches and gasoline. But I thought of our year there and selfishly couldn't do that. That wouldn't hide my crime, only bring more attention to it.

Selfishly. That's a funny word. Everything I did that night was selfish.

I picked up her body and carried it out the front door. It was awkward in my arms, and death seemed to make it heavier. I ended up dragging her. To my left, I saw some pine trees with an opening. My muscles ached as I laid her down in the pine needles. The moon was full, and I could see everything.

I looked at her. Her eyes were open, and the spirits no longer held her body. Her beautiful face, with those clear, intense eyes, stared towards eternity. Her slack mouth told me I did it. I knew I would bury her face down.

I went back to the house and grabbed a shovel. I heard a mournful cry in the distance. Some might have thought it was coyotes, but I knew. It was Catherine. I disobeyed her. I certainly disappointed her. It deflated me and weighed me down even more.

I found the spot and stared at my wife's lifeless face. Her eyes had held such joy—and such terror. I looked at her cheekbones, her lips, and her hair framing her face. Then I remembered that sound she made just before she died—the wet, sickly sound that was her breathing in her death. I leaned over and vomited into the bushes.

I dug all night, my head still pounding from the shovel days before. Just as the sun rose, I came to a spot I knew I would eventually hit. My shovel discarded another mound of dirt. I was bone-tired, so I wasn't moving as fast as I had earlier, and the dirt seemed to slide down the trowel. For some reason, I watched and then saw it—a silky red ribbon, one I had seen Catherine wear so many times. I held it in my hands, not knowing what else I could take—confirmation, warning, revelation … all of it—in this dark and horrible night. Just when I thought there was nothing else, I saw an old letter, folded multiple times. I couldn't believe it had survived all these years, but it had been underneath a large flint rock, which must have covered it well enough to keep it from deteriorating. The letter was covered in blood, dried and very old. I knew what it was … or thought I did. The sun had now given me enough light to read it.

*Dear General Kilpatrick:*

*I fear my letters have been compromised after the disappearance of the Morris girl, who had been quite felicitous in delivering them for me. This, therefore, shall be my last. Please note you must take all appropriate precautions as I was not able to make the special ink that I have on previous occasions.*

*Last night, my husband was again boasting about the designs the turncoats have on your life, again referring to the "Dahlgren-Kilpatrick" affair, laughing at your designs on Richmond. The traitors are your men. This is not a Southern plot. They intend to send some soldiers you do not know Friday next, and among those men, there is one who is skilled in the art of poison. Beyond this, I know nothing, but I do not wish to see ill come to you.*

*I fear my husband believes I am being unfaithful to him. Of course, I am not, but I could understand his logic. My husband was my rock, and even though he too has become a monster (like so many in this war), and even though I now feel I don't even know him, I cannot do anything to bring dishonor to him. Therefore, I shall leave this missive at The Shoals, and I shall not correspond further.*

*I hope this letter finds you well. I pray you may stay that way.*

*Your obedient servant,*

*Catherine Vaughan*

I buried my head in my hands. Catherine had not been having an affair; she had been trying to save General Kilpatrick. That was her connection to The Shoals; she was trying to complete the task life had not allowed.

She was just a couple hundred yards from delivering the message. I could see her, bravely climbing the hill, one last task before her conscience would let her rest. And there before her was a dead-eyed northern soldier, who cut her off, knowing her intentions. She kneeled, shaking, trembling, praying for mercy from a traitorous soldier, who would lose his life that night too although they would find his body months later and still upright. He ran his sword through her and threw her in a shallow grave, burying the last note with her.

I was glad the letter existed, and I took it with me as I returned to the house for the final time. I spread it out and put it on the kitchen table, hoping it would be understood and maybe help free Catherine from her eternal delivery.

I knew I wouldn't be around. I stood and marveled at how much blood had flown from Leah, how clear it was what had happened. I left that place, looking around as if I expected the posse to already be on the way, and went back into the forest. I know they'll find me eventually. May God have mercy on my soul.

# CHAPTER 32

*Dear Michael:*

*I feel like a girl getting ready for prom.*

*When I started writing, I didn't think about the bestseller lists. I just thought of the feeling of walking into a bookstore and seeing my title up there on the shelf. Don't get me wrong, I have plenty of pride in Southern Gothic and what the store has become, but there's something about seeing my name there. It probably doesn't seem like a big deal to you. But to me, it means everything.*

*These weeks of mystery and surprise and romance have been the nicest of my adult life. I appreciate your honesty and humor and the way you look at me. You have made me feel like every day is prom and every night is a promise. I am so excited to ride up to see this magical place, to feel the setting, to understand the land. I can't wait. I don't know if I'll be able to sleep.*

*You're out on your walk, soaking in the sights and sounds of my town. I'd like for it to become yours. When we return, if you want to move in, under your conditions (given your peculiar circumstances), you're invited. I want to share more of our lives. I hope you'll take me up on this. It is not easy to offer. Lance made me wary about how lame most relationships become. You have already restored my faith in men. Thank you for that.*

*Yours,*

***M***

# RED RIBBON

## EPILOGUE

The greatest thing for a fugitive in Georgia is the number of tree-covered acres. Not the occasional shade tree, but heavily wooded, Lewis and Clark-type acreage. We were so secluded already; I figured it would take at least a week before anyone came looking. I thought about getting in the car, driving south to Key West, and seeing how long I could make it there, bar tending or doing some such thing, but that wouldn't work. I still held out for a visit from Catherine, a haunting from Leah, something to connect me to the bright past I chose to leave behind. No, I was here for the duration, another haunted soul to join the ghosts.

I found a cave so far back in the woods I was pretty sure snakes couldn't find it. It was cool in the day and warm at night, and I thought I could make it through the winter. I like being close to the deeds I did. I have been here ever since, spending my days replaying that endless string of what-ifs and my nights hearing those haunting sounds, the ones they describe in books. Now I understand. Someday I will be one of them. These are the tortured souls who ventured too far, who chose to live in the shroud of mystery, for whom one life wasn't enough. Sometimes they visit and sit with me a while, and some, like Catherine, can only be heard in the distance. She's mad at me, and I understand why. I couldn't follow her one request.

I don't know if ghosts move on or if their torment is eternal. I chose her. I didn't kill for her, but everyone would think I did. And now she hides from me. I chose to spend eternity with her even if I have to wait. Even if my punishment for my misdeeds is eternal separation.

I can hear Leah too. Her cries are more tortured, and I want to tear my ears out when I hear her. My guilt is unrelenting. My remorse is complete. Sometimes I hear her talking and arguing with someone, sometimes a man, sometimes a woman. I fear Leah's anger, and yet, I deserve it. Leah made it hard to love her, but I made a vow, and I betrayed that vow in more ways than any man I know.

There are times I dream of forgiveness, for the soft touch of grace, or for some sort of mercy that rises above all of this. But I don't think I could live outside of the prison I've built for myself, one where the past is all that matters, where the souls you've touched are close enough to be constant reminders.

If I am ever found, they will have to acquit me in court because I'm sure they'd find me insane. I know I could walk into any sheriff's office, tell my tale, and live out my days in the relative comfort of the loony bin because the truth is just too crazy for anyone to genuinely believe. I know I wouldn't have believed it before I landed in the middle of it.

But I can't leave this place. If they find me, they'll have to kill me. Because I'm waiting for her. I want to feel her touch my lips and peer into my soul. I don't know if I'm ever going to get the chance until I become one of them, haunted in death the way I am in life. I know that's where I'm heading.

As of now, that's all I'm really waiting for.

# PART II
# PURGATORY

"If one advances confidently in the direction of his dreams, and endeavors to live the life which he has imagined, he will meet with a success unexpected in common hours."

—Henry David Thoreau

# CHAPTER 33

Broderick Yancey hadn't started out this way. His business had been highly successful. He married a beautiful woman and had three fantastic kids. All of them went to good schools. Patrick graduated at the top of his class at the University of the South in Sewanee, Randall aced medical school at Chapel Hill, and his lovely Quinn was all set to spend her last year at Emory and then move on to her lifelong dream of working on Capitol Hill.

Then that man came. That narcissistic bastard. That wife-deserting, party-throwing, affected author bastard. Quinn didn't stand a chance. Michael Black, who could have picked on someone his own size, would instead come over and eat holiday meals with them, shake Broderick's hand, and pretend it wasn't strange to date a college girl twenty-five years his junior.

He warned her. He didn't want to dictate his daughter's life. But something about the man wasn't right. He saw it from a mile away. And it hadn't done a damn bit of good.

She called that Saturday night and told him she was meeting Michael. Broderick had to be both parents to little Quinn since his wife died of breast cancer seven years earlier, and in moments like that one, he missed her the most. She would have known what to say. She could have made it better. Maybe she could have stopped Quinn from making such a foolish mistake. Instead, he caved and told her to call him the next morning. The call never came.

They never found any evidence, but a father knows the truth in his soul—at least one body was buried somewhere in Georgia. If he needed more proof, Michael's disappearance said it all. He hoped Michael still walked this earth so he could kill him with his own hands. He wouldn't hesitate. He knew his sons would do the same if they were given the chance.

Michael Black—and Quinn's "disappearance"—had turned Broderick into a tense and angry man. He tried to play golf, meet his friends for drinks, and focus on his work, but his mind always returned to the black chasm of his daughter's disappearance. What had that man put her through? What were her last words, her last thoughts before he squeezed the life out of her?

The emergence of Michael Black's star pupil into the national spotlight poured salt on his wounds. The entire country raved about Meredith Harper's book. Every article and every newscast made note of her close connection to Michael Black. He couldn't stand it.

Flipping through the morning news shows, he switched the channel to MSNBC, and there she sat again, being interviewed by Candice Mackenzie, talking about Michael's influence on her as a writer. Dammit. He knew Michael Black was still alive, knew he lurked out there somewhere. Call it a father's intuition.

He took out his Michael Black file and made some notes. It had been a long time since he'd visited Savannah.

# Chapter 34

Meredith had made the trip to The Shoals with Michael. He had described the old plantation remarkably well in *Red Ribbon.* Although they couldn't go in because someone lived there, Meredith measured out the steps to the graves in the book and, to her great happiness, found nothing that looked remotely like a burial spot. Michael rolled his eyes through the entire trip. He acted insulted by the insinuation, but he was a good sport about it. She floated back to Savannah amid publishing fantasies.

After Michael got over his hurt feelings, he gave her the game plan. He had wanted to send her to his agent, Lisa Haglund, but decided it would be too obvious. And besides, she knew him too well. They settled on Allen Mattson, a young, up-and-coming agent known for representing debut authors with blockbuster potential. Michael helped her write the query letter. He concocted a story involving Meredith's involvement with Michael before his disappearance. It worked. Allen secured an advance of $250,000 by setting up a bidding war between rival publishers. In the end, Gandolfo-Griffie, former home of Michael's novels, won. Publicists played up her connection with Michael, the famous author who disappeared under mysterious circumstances, and as Labor Day rolled around—almost a year after Meredith's first encounter with Michael—*Red Ribbon* was poised to launch as a bestseller.

She got to see Michael occasionally. They had tried to set up a somewhat normal living arrangement, but it hadn't worked for either of them. She was used to living alone, and Michael was going crazy having to stay in one place. Sometimes she went weeks without hearing from him, almost long enough to convince her he wasn't coming back. In those times, Meredith missed him. She missed his body—his lovemaking had a manic energy she found irresistible—and she missed talking with him about books, those she'd read, their own novel, and the whole publication process.

When the critics declared *Red Ribbon* a book worthy of award consideration, it was a *fait accompli.* Her book—it had her plot after all—was going to be huge. Allen had even started talking to film scouts. The whole experience didn't seem real.

Her publicist booked her on *Charlie Rose* and *All Things Considered. Vanity Fair* asked to do a spread about the bookstore and her novel. More and more, book-related commitments pulled her away from the day-to-day running of Southern Gothic, so she gave Nate a five percent stake. As the day moved closer to do the official first book signing—at her store, of course—she was practically floating.

Of course, in Meredith's mind, everything reminded her the story was hers, but the rest of the book was not. All she heard circled around the ease of the prose and the stately setting. As long as this book proved the only source of her fame, Meredith would never be able to outrun Michael's involvement.

She scheduled the signing for the afternoon—plenty of time for the Georgia churchgoers to finish services and brunch. She slept late, and then took a long, relaxing bath before getting ready for her debut. She thought about wearing something formal, a dress with heels, but then decided last minute to go with jeans and a blouse. She didn't have to dress up for these people. They knew her.

She got a text from her agent.

```
Allen: Sorry. Had a family emergency. Can't make it
☹
Meredith: Oh no!
Allen: You go sell some books. We'll have plenty of
time for celebration later.
```

Not even Allen's absence could get her down today. She jumped in her car to head to brunch at the Funky Brunch Cafe, not far from her store on Broughton Street, when she thought of something. She hadn't left her driveway yet, so she threw the car in park, got out, and came around to the passenger side. She expected people to bring flowers and gifts, and she thought it would make sense to bring a couple of extra boxes.

Meredith flipped on the overhead light and started humming "A Case of You," the Joni Mitchell song running through her head. She saw several boxes she had brought from the store in the back corner. She looked up at the naked light bulb and thought she needed to work on this place—it felt a bit creepy.

She decided two big boxes would do the trick. She grabbed one and tossed it towards the car. Then she reached for the second.

She noticed the smell first, a warm blast of alcohol—the way her grandpa smelled after returning from "going outside" as he called it. She looked behind the box and froze. There, on the ground in front of her, a man slept, breathing in a labored manner. She wanted to turn and scream, but she felt pretty sure he hadn't sensed her presence. Her breaths grew shallow, and the blood rushed through her ears.

She heard a loud *pop* above her and couldn't help but gasp. She bent so far forward, studying the scene, she nearly fell right on top of him. The man didn't even stir. She realized the aluminum roof was just expanding and calmed herself.

By then, she had a sinking suspicion. Oh, don't let it be true. The man had his hand across his face, probably protecting himself from sunlight, but the jacket gave him away. Her lover, her hero, the man who inspired her was stone-cold passed out just feet from her bed, where she would have welcomed him with kisses and the gift of her body. She wanted to make this something explainable—maybe he had drunk too much and couldn't make it inside. But when she widened her gaze, she saw the extent of his nest: a sleeping bag, dog-eared paperbacks from her library, a Mag flashlight, a bottle of Absinthe—and a man in such an altered state her appearance and bumbling hadn't even stirred him. He was used to sleeping there.

Meredith, no longer afraid he would stir, sat on the floor and tried to breathe around the awful stench. Who the hell was she dealing with?

There would be no time for brunch. She had to start over, fixing her face for this momentous day—with the knowledge her hero was nothing like what she had convinced herself to believe.

# CHAPTER 35

The scene at the store could fulfill any author's dream. Although she had imagined this moment her entire life, her stomach rebelled. She felt woozy and uninterested.

She plastered a smile and surveyed her surroundings. The crowd had spilled outside, and the atmosphere felt more like a football game or rock concert than a book signing. The women still wore their church hats, and the men had dressed smartly in blazers and loafers. And of course, her friends were already there. Terrie and Jennifer served punch and poured wine, and Lisa walked around with cocktail shrimp. The place buzzed with excitement.

But she couldn't get him out of her head. Before she left for the store, she tried one more time to wake the bastard up, but he didn't so much as crack an eyelid. He obviously hadn't showered in who knows how long. Christ, he'd probably been pissing in there, too. How could she not take it personally? The jackass preferred sleeping in a dank nest to her bed.

She immediately accepted the red wine Nate handed her and had her second glass almost before he walked away. After downing her third, her nerves returned to some semblance of normalcy.

Since she had made the bargain with him, she had cut her life into small pieces. Now she needed that skill just to make it through this party. She had stifled the scary part because he fed her the dreams she so desperately wanted.

Meredith realized she really didn't know much about Michael's past. Could some bad series of events have brought him to this point? Mental illness? Alcohol? There must be a logical explanation.

She tried to shake her mind from such things. She needed to soak up the joy of this moment. She needed to be present.

Meredith thought about people who got swept up, whose lives got out of control. When did Monica Lewinsky know her life was ruined? What was the exact moment? When did Nixon know he was going down? They had to keep the mask on, keep moving forward. Meredith now had no idea what she did and didn't know. When her hairdresser asked her to sign a book, she thought she might burst into tears.

# CHAPTER 36

In the middle of the first group of hopeful fans, many of whom seemed to frequent the bookstore, stood Broderick Yancey. He had come to buy the book, scan it for clues, and help him in his search. He also came to meet Meredith.

He hoped Michael Black would show. For years, he had stared at his picture, willing it to speak. Sometimes he felt more familiar with him than his own children. He peered around the room. He knew Michael was too smart to show up, but it didn't hurt to keep an eye out.

He arrived early enough to browse the bookstore uninterrupted. He took in the bookshelves, the posters, the signs, the café. By the looks of it, Meredith had gotten carried away with hero worship, not just of Michael, but of so many others.

Broderick occasionally read, maybe once or twice a year, but he didn't understand this adulation of the written word. Perhaps he judged too much because the book fetish led many people to protect his daughter's abductor. Even on the message boards to this day, people continued to respect Michael because he could write well.

Meredith sat down at the signing table by the bakery, huge stacks of books piled on either side of her. Her assistant handed her a pen and a glass of wine. Despite himself, Broderick liked her. She had an effortless beauty. He noticed she was a little more reserved at first but then seemed to ease into the role of local celebrity. She touched people when they talked to her, gently emphasizing her words and making them feel comfortable. She met their eyes and smiled with hers.

He sensed Michael was involved in a much deeper way; he had shared her bed the way he had Quinn's. He noticed a scar on her right arm, right above the wrist, and wondered if Michael had put it there. As he got closer to her, he felt his throat go dry. He wanted to go to her. At times like this, Broderick realized he played a game that could never have a winner, never satisfy what had been burned out of him. He wanted to pull this woman aside and interrogate her. But it would serve no purpose, so he would simply buy a book. He couldn't stomach the thought of having her sign it. He didn't want to like her. She belonged to Michael. He paid for his book, and before he got his change, he hit the door and disappeared into the winter sunlight.

# Chapter 37

Michael woke up some time after one. He looked around and noticed the boxes strewn around; he realized Meredith had found him out. It disappointed him he hadn't been coherent for the confrontation. That would have been half the fun. He noticed a note resting on top of one of the boxes, scrawled in Meredith's loopy handwriting.

*Be gone when I get home.*

He had hoped for more vitriol, something mean and nasty he could think about late at night, but this woman was a jewel, and no matter what else transpired, she would never be able to stop loving him—or at least his writing. He counted on it—and the fact he could now prove she had duped the entire American public.

Early on, Michael had seen the relationship as a panacea, something that could do away with all of his flaws as if Meredith's magic would make him normal again. When it didn't happen, he blamed her.

She lived a happy, naïve existence. She had so many questions about the corners of his universe—the characters he created, the stories he forgot, the minutiae of a well-chronicled life of writing. She wanted to know him and be with him. She didn't believe the other Michael existed, or she chose to look the other way when confronted with any evidence. Problem was this was the real Michael—the one Meredith had no chance of changing.

He knew this day would come. He hadn't specifically intended it to be today, but he loved that she would hate him all the more for it. His plan had been to hide out until 5 or 6 p.m. and then pretend like he had just come back into town, take her out for a celebratory dinner, and end the night in her bed. He had been away from her for two weeks, spending the last six nights in his lair. He needed a nice long bath and some time between her legs. But last night, he wound up at a bar downtown, drinking absinthe and thinking despicable thoughts—thoughts of putting nails through her hands, branding her … He didn't like when those thoughts came, so he kept drinking. When he fell into his space around 4 a.m., he slept in a different corner of the universe, one without any communication with the surface world.

Early on, Michael made keys to everything. Of course, Meredith had no idea. He thought she would likely change the locks now. Most people would under similar circumstances. He didn't want to make it look as if he had free access to her house, so he shoved his simple note in the frame of the back door.

*email: pupil75@hushmail.com*

*password: southernbelle72*

He put the rest of his impromptu home on his back and headed out.

Michael turned and tried to memorize the house. He would be back, but he had no idea how long it would be. He blew a kiss at Meredith's bedroom window. Goodbye, he mouthed. I'll see you again. Then he walked west and didn't look back.

# CHAPTER 38

Broderick left the book signing and had plans of heading home to Atlanta. It would take a little over three hours, and he could make it back in time to watch the Sunday night NFL game. But first he had a stop to make.

He made the short drive to her house and parked half a block away.

Broderick rang the front bell and, after a few seconds, tried the handle. As he expected, no one was home. He walked around the back door and peered through the window.

Broderick scolded himself. What was he doing snooping in her backyard? He wasn't a detective. As he turned to leave, a folded paper, stuck in the frame of the backdoor, caught his attention. It was probably nothing, but it wouldn't hurt to take a quick look.

When he saw the password, his heart caught in his throat. He had been through his daughter's papers enough to recognize the handwriting anywhere. He took a picture of the note with his phone and did his best to replace it exactly as it was left. He had to stop himself from dancing all the way back to the car. He had the first actual lead on Michael Black in years.

# Chapter 39

At the store, the line to sign books never ended, and Meredith's hand began to cramp. People milled about, drinking and talking. But she couldn't take her mind off Michael.

She noticed Jennifer motioning to her. Meredith apologized to a store regular and finally broke away to speak to one of her best and oldest friends.

Jennifer grabbed her by the hand and took her just outside the store and into the late-afternoon sunlight.

Meredith wondered if something was wrong. Had she found out? All of a sudden, the afternoon's glimmer faded away.

"I read my copy last night." Jennifer had a mix of buoyance and excitement in her voice. "I just love it. It reminds me of all the books we used to read together." There were tears welling in her eyes. "I'm just so happy you stayed with it. I didn't know if you would after the bookstore and all. You've added your name to that list we all would like to join, and I'm so proud of you."

Meredith hugged her friend. Jennifer was right—Meredith was finally doing what she always wanted to do. She had turned her dreams into reality. She did her best to push down the nagging feeling of guilt.

As the afternoon wound down, her thoughts shifted back to

Michael—the mildewed smell of his nest, the dirt and dust he chose to sleep in, the stink of alcohol on his breath. It was not an impromptu landing spot, but somewhere he spent time. The hairs stood up on the back of her neck. She felt equal parts of revulsion and fear.

The terror of the phone calls, the harsh words he sometimes left at her feet, the moments when all the praise in the world couldn't distract him from a dark mood—she couldn't ignore the other side of him anymore. She shuddered as she thought of the nights they had spent together and the way she had felt safe in his arms. Which man was he? She wanted to wretch. She turned around and scanned the room for Nate.

Luckily, she caught sight of him speaking with the mayor of Savannah, a regular customer at the store, and Scott Pettit, one of the Savannah's finest criminal lawyers and Meredith's longtime friend.

Meredith tugged at Nate's elbow. "Can you follow me home?" she asked, hoping she came across sober enough so it wouldn't sound like a come-on.

If Nate thought that, it didn't show. "What's wrong?" Concern filled his eyes. Too much concern.

She briefly regretted asking him. "I'm sure it's fine, but I heard some things last night, and I just wouldn't mind if you would help me get in okay." She wasn't scared, but the whole thing made her want to burst into tears.

"No problem," he said.

Since her impromptu courting lesson, Nate had seemed to move on from his crush and had been out with a few women. She hadn't met them yet, but sometimes he would ask advice, and Meredith happily dished it. She hoped she was not putting him back on her trail.

Meredith pulled around to the carriage house and got out of the car gingerly. She could see Michael hadn't cleaned up the mess, so she made sure to direct Nate away from it. She looked carefully around the boxes to make sure he wasn't hiding.

"What did you hear? Something like the last time?" Nate asked.

She shook her head. "It was probably nothing. If you'll just get me inside, I'm sure I'll be fine."

Nate took the lead around the back and noticed the paper before she did. He grabbed it and started to open it when Meredith realized what it likely was.

She pushed up next to Nate, her breasts brushing against him. "I'll take that. Thanks, Nate."

"What is it?"

"Nothing. I asked my neighbor to check too, so I think it's just his report." She quickly slipped it into her pocket. "Do you hear anything?" she asked.

Neither of them said anything. A big gust of sea air made the branches creak and sway overhead.

Nate shook his head. "I don't."

She knew he spooked easily and wanted to get out of there. Frankly, she did too. "Thanks, Nate." She kissed him on the cheek. She hoped it would keep him off-guard all the way home.

She smiled as she saw from his look, it had done just that.

# CHAPTER 40

The brilliance and happiness of the afternoon starkly contrasted with the evening's darkness. She checked to see if anything looked out of place and then went to the kitchen and poured herself a glass of her favorite, La Crema Pinot. The burn in the back of her throat calmed her and gave her the courage she needed. She pulled the note back out of her pocket. The password he gave her, southernbelle72, was a combination of his pet name for her and the year of her birth. He continued his toying with her, even now.

Meredith was not only suffering from the shock of finding Michael in an unconscious mess on her garage floor, but from a broken heart as well. She had spent the last year convinced Michael would come out of the shadows, restore his name, and be her husband. How stupid could she be? He was comfortable where he was—in those shadows, in those hiding places. He liked that life. What did it say about her that she couldn't see him for what he was?

Meredith moved around the house carefully, expecting him to walk in and pretend like today never happened. She could feel him there. She felt disgusted and used. Yet she still wanted to see him.

Her phone lit up with several emails from Allen, who had solidified what looked to be a marvelous week ahead. She would be doing a cooking show with Bobby Flay and a sit-down interview with Bob Edwards. Now that she was experienced in thinking of herself in the role of author, the job got easier and easier. They were putting her up at The Plaza—another bucket list item checked off.

For the most part, the trappings of her newfound fame were marvelous. But she still had moments, usually late at night, when a sinking feeling consumed her. *She had taken credit for a book she didn't write.*

An hour later, finally convinced he had left, she sat in her bathtub and cried.

# CHAPTER 41

The email came four days later. Meredith stared at it for a full minute before finally opening.

> Hi.

That was all master22@hushmail.com had sent.

Meredith sat in her hotel room at The Plaza in New York. It was unreal. She had almost managed to push the events of the past week to the side and just enjoy this energy high doing signings at bookstores and talking to news shows. Between the day's two events, she climbed into a limo and decided she needed to respond. She shook so badly she could barely compose anything.

"You okay, ma'am?" The driver furrowed his brow in concern.

"Too much coffee. I'll be fine."

She pulled herself together and typed out her response.

> Dear "Master,"
>
> I was surprised to find your unusual sleeping arrangement. It stings a little to know sleeping in a cardboard box is preferable to sharing my bed.

> I think you need to find another pupil. Let's both keep our secrets and leave it at that. There are things both of us need concealed.
>
> Pupil

It surprised her how much it bothered her to send the email, how much it hurt to cut the cord, to say goodbye to the warmth of his body and the heights of their passion. She couldn't tell anyone how it tore at a part of her to let him go. A part of her loved the drama and the roller coaster ride. But she couldn't sacrifice anything else. She was sure of it.

Meredith needed Michael as much as Michael needed her. But she also couldn't spend the rest of her life looking over her shoulder and worrying about where he slept at night. He needed to stay hidden to keep his freedom *and* to ensure the success of her career.

As soon as the *whoosh* of the sent email hit her ears, she regretted it. If he took it the wrong way, she could be closer to, not further from, mutually assured destruction. She didn't know this man, or maybe she hoped she didn't. Maybe this was all passing madness. She longed for that. She hoped she hadn't just made things much worse.

Now she would simply have to wait.

# CHAPTER 42

She spent her last day in New York worrying. Was he going to respond red-hot with anger or have an icy calm? But it was worse—she heard nothing at all. She had an important meeting with *The New Yorker* about a piece they were going to do, and she saw the frown on the writer's face when she anxiously checked her phone every few minutes.

She took the train to Boston the next morning and went into the same routine. At one point, a good-looking man bumped against her, and she nearly screamed. She needed to see a doctor, but she knew she wouldn't—or couldn't.

The publisher put Meredith up in a suite befitting royalty at the Mandarin Oriental in Boston. The gray street view turned into magic when she entered the vast lobby. She tried to soak in every second of her momentary royal status, appreciating the sculptures and modern lines of the hotel. The last book signing had been packed, and several people said nice things about what she had written online about Michael. She welcomed hearing nice things for a change. She had worried about everything that had been said and wondered if rumors held some truth. Oddly, having someone else stick up for him felt like a huge burden had been lifted.

*Red Ribbon* debuted at number three on the New York Times bestseller list. *Number three.* She couldn't believe it. She stared at the listing, just below John Grisham. She thought about calling Terrie or Jennifer to *ooh* and *ah*, but she had been too consumed with worry over the unanswered email and feared they would pick up the edge in her voice.

She went to a nice dinner with her Boston press contact and devoured the oysters and crab legs. The woman loved the book and predicted great things. Meredith wished she could focus on the praise, but her mind had left the conversation. They walked back by Faneuil Hall, and in the noisy darkness of the city, she said her goodbyes and found herself alone with her thoughts. She lingered in the lobby for a moment, postponing the dread of looking at her email yet again, but finally decided to head to her room. She climbed under the covers and stared at the glittering skyline outside her window.

Then, just hours after the greatest news of her life, he emailed her.

She held her breath as she read.

Dear Pupil:

Should I even call you that? You read my books all those years and never learned to write. Maybe I should have chosen "Straw Man" as an email address instead. Seems more appropriate. Lucky Straw Man.

We need to get a couple things straight in this relationship—WHO GIVES THE THREATS and WHO SITS AROUND COWERING IN FUCKING TERROR WHEN THEY GET THEM. I am Rumpelstiltskin, and you are the pretty princess who hopes I spin gold for her at night. You better remember because there is plenty of peasant work in the kingdom. You like the Mandarin, eh? I have friends every single place you go. They don't give a shit about my past, and they WILL give me your itinerary and room number (1425) when I ask them to. Since I pay them more than their annual salary, they're happy to oblige.

I can write anything here because YOU won't do anything about it. You can't go to the police and tell them your blood stalker told you he knows about the black vibrator you keep in the Steve Madden box third from the left in your closet. Or that he smiled and licked it when he found it. Or how he found his way into your duct work and looked down over you while you were sleeping.

Your blood stalker is trying to cool his anger and not punish you for the way you are behaving. Your blood stalker will sleep in your garage if he chooses.

All those things are now on the table. You have a beautiful life. I won't even object if you take a lover. It might turn me on. But you WILL know I am in charge, and you are very lucky to be where you are.

Your devoted friend,

Master

# Chapter 43

The email knocked the wind out of her.

She read and re-read it. She didn't want to, but she couldn't stop. She felt like she had read one book only to find at the end it had transformed into something entirely different. He could be making up the stuff about the air ducts—she remembered that from one of Patterson's early books—but he got her vibrator's hiding place right. She couldn't imagine the shame of turning back at this point. The sullen stares of the customers, the unmet eyes of her friends. No, she had made her Kafka nightmare. Now she had to watch herself become the roach.

Meredith hoped his desire to stay hidden—and keep the truth that way too—was as strong in him as it was in her. Maybe mutually assured destruction could work here as well. If he did her in, she would sure as hell take him down too.

Sleep crept in, with strange, oppressive dreams. Michael at the foot of her bed. Michael walking with her down a long hall. Michael's face hovering over hers as she slept, his breath rancid on her cheeks. When she woke, she saw a stream of light from the window and felt more tired than ever.

She dragged herself into the bathroom to turn on the shower. On the mirror, someone had written a message in a woman's flowery handwriting using her own lipstick, a blood red shade.

*I didn't write Red Ribbon. - M.H.*

# Chapter 44

Meredith grabbed a towel and tried to wipe away the message. Instead, she just smeared the lipstick across the surface. She stopped to look at herself through the mirror's red haze.

She looked like she had been crumpled up. She could not see herself as heroic or even okay. She appeared frazzled and disheartened and desperate. The early days of the bookstore seemed halcyon and so very distant.

She texted the organizers to say she couldn't make it to the TV appearance. She didn't want to see or talk to anyone. She flung the curtains wide and decided she would not be an author that day. She turned on the trashiest daytime television, emptied the vodka from the minibar straight into her mouth, followed by the whiskey, and then got under the covers.

As she dozed, she suddenly realized she had lulled herself again into a false sense of security. One of Michael's *people* had a key to her suite. Or Michael could be here right now, watching her. It was time for some fresh air.

She got ready, put on a jacket, and left the hotel shortly before eleven. She headed toward the Back Bay and tried to keep all her crises straight—not an easy task.

Meredith could simply go home. Rent a house until she could buy a new one. Become a modern day Harper Lee, living off her single bestseller forever. There were much worse literary fates. She liked the prospect better than writing a bad second book.

Meredith had started toying with a new book idea. She wanted to have it in Allen's hands as soon as possible, but the writing had been slow and tedious, and she second-guessed herself at every point. The first few chapters pleased her, but she still had no idea where the story would end. Her efforts had been tenuous at best.

Southern Gothic could keep her satisfied. Michael wasn't exactly credible right now, and if he popped up, who would believe him? She would distance herself from him completely, heart be damned.

The cold and blustery air refreshed her as she walked through the markets and bought some trinkets for friends, feeling light and free after her decision. She had some pizza at Pappa Razzi's and thoroughly enjoyed herself until she saw the familiar red type.

A complete stranger clutched a copy of her book. The scene sent her soaring.

# CHAPTER 45

Meredith soldiered on. She decided she could always cancel if she needed to but went ahead with the tour. Things went well in Philadelphia and Chicago, and she blew the roof off Austin and Dallas. She got drunk, stayed at nice hotels, and people treated her like a queen. In Los Angeles, she sat down with the producer Allen hoped would sign onto the movie project. By then, Michael had backed off; he'd sent conciliatory emails and flowers. It turned her stomach.

The book continued to perform incredibly well. It moved to Number One on the *Times* list and stayed there for five weeks. Meredith would look at the daily sales printouts and marvel at the money coming her way.

But she still wasn't going to write another book—one decision she stuck to. But she decided to continue the book tour, giving up on it would be giving in too easy. She deserved to have some fun after all Michael had put her through.

The bookstore was doing great under the combination of Nate's hands-on management and her increased celebrity. When she was in town, she signed dozens and dozens of books, a process she had grown to detest. Weekly, she would get the same email from the store:

Autographed copies sold out. Come in and replenish.

But Meredith knew if she didn't follow up with another book fairly quickly, she would be doing many more signings at the store—what a letdown that would be after the whirlwind of the last year. At the moment, however, it was better than the alternative—publish a bad book and be forgotten. Her attempt at a new book, *Creeping Vines*, wasn't where she wanted it to be, and she realized even attempting anything was a continuing contradiction. She wasn't even close. She kept trying, and the book kept resisting. She felt like her instincts were proving her right.

Even though it would have made her year any other time, Meredith now dreaded telling Allen she would turn down the offer to publish another book. She would simply say she wanted a clear idea of what she would write before committing to anything. Allen, she assumed, would find this idea laughable, as she too would have before this experience. Turning down a book deal contradicted everything she had ever believed in. But then again, she would also have been against plagiarism. She thought about studying up on Marlowe and Shakespeare but decided that would depress her way too much.

Allen didn't reach out for a while, since working on the book release in other languages consumed most of his already busy schedule.

Meredith decided to stay an extra week in Los Angeles and enjoy the warm, sunny days and cool nighttime breezes. There, she could almost imagine a future without a blood stalker.

But as always, reality caught up. Michael sent emails asking questions about everything. He told her of his displeasure over her spending less time at home. She tried to ignore him, but that turned out to be just as stressful as actually dealing with him.

Obviously, she didn't want to go back to her house. Michael could be lurking in her closet or peering over her from the air ducts. Instead, she booked a room at a hotel.

When she finally got back to Savannah, she planned to put her house on the market and hunt for a new place. She went to the store most days and interacted with customers, but through his watchful gaze—and she assumed he watched all the time—he would be able to tell, even if she never wrote again, he had changed her life in every way. She reached out to a real estate agent to list her house and help her find a new one. She tried to make everything go back to normal, but she could never shake the feeling Michael always lurked in the shadows, watching her every move.

Meredith lived off the revenue from Southern Gothic and the advance from *Red Ribbon*, but she had yet to see a royalty check. She asked Allen about this, but he told her not to worry. The advance on the movie option didn't amount to much despite the book's success because Allen strongly suggested taking a better back-end position. At least, she knew she could stay in a hotel for as long as she needed to.

Then, about three weeks after she returned to Savannah and with the book still at the top of the charts, the call came. Allen phoned from New York with sunlight in his voice. Her publisher had offered a $1.5 million advance on the next book!

She took a deep breath, then another, and then told him she would have to think about it. She hung up on her agent, and she knew he would be sorely confused.

# CHAPTER 46

Online, in the Michael Black forums, Broderick adopted the name The Father. He didn't say much, but what he did say made everyone listen. There had been many theories about Meredith's book and whether it held clues to Quinn's disappearance—especially with its fatal ending.

At Broderick's behest, the sheriff had agreed to bring a couple of dogs to The Shoals, and Broderick let himself hope they'd find something. But the dogs hadn't even so much as picked up a scent; apparently, the burial site in *Red Ribbon* was fictional.

The Sherriff had managed to keep the whole thing secret. Part of Broderick felt relieved they hadn't found anything. Without a body, he could imagine the possibility Quinn still lived.

After Broderick saw the emails, he paid an English professor to analyze and compare the few pieces of Meredith's writing he could find online to Michael Black's novels and *Red Ribbon*. The professor believed there was a much greater chance Michael wrote the book than Meredith had a literary transformation. But it was probably just tweed jacket speculation confirming what he wanted to hear.

One night around Valentine's Day, when a light dusting of snow had come to the northern half of Georgia and after the law of gravity had finally pulled *Red Ribbon* off the very top of the chart, Broderick wandered back online to see if anything new had developed.

He liked Meredith's website best, actually. She gave room for all opinions, including ones she clearly wouldn't have liked. He had to give her credit for that. She allowed even the darkest of the anti-Michael voices, like BlackPlague, to speak.

> BlackPlague. 2/12/17. 5:54 p.m.
>
> Go back and read the very first fricking paragraph of Red Ribbon. I can't believe I missed it:
>
> > *There was a time when nothing in my life was as it seemed. Up was down, left was right, backwards and frontwards chased each other's tails right in front of me. I was a lonely man, and I buried more loves, literally and figuratively, than anyone should ever have to.*
>
> Say what you want to about Mr. Black—I know what I'd like to say—but he's a fantastic writer. This is a good book by anyone's standards. But that's not a strong opening. If I were his editor, I'd tell him to go sit his ass back down until he came up with something better. So, what if it's not really meant to advance the plot? What if it's a clue? What happens if the front of the house is the back, every right is left, and vice versa? What do you find?

Broderick's heart pounded. He picked up the phone and dialed the sheriff's number.

# CHAPTER 47

The howling wind cut through them all, including Broderick. He cursed himself for not wearing a warmer jacket. He gazed across the field to the group of people huddled together, their backs to the wind. There were a few curious residents and a couple of deputies. Broderick feared what they would find, but living the rest of his life without any answers scared him more.

Broderick gave the sheriff the map he made by turning all the directions within the book upside down and backwards. It pointed to a general area to start.

The property owners came outside to watch, just as they had the first time. The success of the novel had started drawing crowds, and instead of being upset about it, they embraced it and charged for tours. If they succeeded today, Broderick doubted they would enjoy it much longer, but in cynical moments, he knew the specter of death would only add to their macabre attraction.

Just a few yards further than he anticipated, the dogs found their mark. They barked, started digging, and ran in frenzied circles. Their handlers tugged on their leashes. Broderick knew. He didn't need those dumb dogs or those guys in suits with their DNA kits to tell him. He wished his boys were there. But they had succeeded in moving on in a way he had never been able to.

As the deputies began to dig, Broderick held his head in his hands. He found no solace in learning the truth—just a new bottom of despair.

# CHAPTER 48

The body found buried at The Shoals was all over the news. Reverse the directions and find the grave. Much speculating went on about what would happen next, but everyone assumed Michael was guilty, and Meredith knew it. Worse still, she helped him stay hidden, aiding and abetting a murderer.

Perhaps most interesting to Meredith, who couldn't bear to watch but felt she had to, was the fact no one accused her of not writing the book. The public thought Michael influenced her, thought maybe she had been his lover, but they didn't really explore the idea she wasn't the creator.

Meredith was a bundle of nerves. She missed Michael, as crazy as that sounded. She had come to consider their uneven and scary cipher as a real relationship. She depended on him emotionally and physically. She knew she didn't want him back, but she missed the part he played in her life, and no one had replaced him. Only he understood everything—only he knew all her secrets.

Michael had killed Quinn. Maybe she had gotten in the way, or maybe Quinn knew the real Michael, the one Meredith now saw. But Meredith wasn't Quinn. She was older and wiser. She meant more to

Michael; Michael said so.

Very likely, she would be charged with murder. Dear God, how did she find herself here?

# Chapter 49

Scott Roberts Pettit was three years older than Meredith. They became friends in high school, but then again, Scott befriended everyone. With a smile always on his face, anyone could feel comfortable around him.

Scott's father, Walt, had been a business attorney, long representing shrimping interests and setting up generation-skipping trusts for the wealthy of the marshes. After spending a little time as an assistant prosecutor, Scott won several massive cases no one expected him to win, which brought him to the attention of the right people, and his career took off.

Meredith wouldn't have labeled him a close friend, but she always loved running into him on River Street or catching him having a slice of pizza at Vinnie Van Go's. He listened well, told wonderful stories about his cases, and gave his time freely. When she needed a divorce, he had recommended his friend John Cowherd, who had done everything but spank Lance on the behind before he finished with him. Naturally, in the days following the discovery of Quinn Yancey's body, Scott would be the first person she contacted.

The office was an old row house he had bought with his father twenty-five years before. Its décor—dark wood furniture, lots of leather, and musty old books—spoke of understated power. It was as traditional as you could find but manned with people who somehow hadn't let their positions ruin who they were.

Scott sat down in his office on Taylor Street and tried to convince her not to hire him.

"I think you need to get someone you don't know," Scott said.

"Why would I want to do that?"

"Because we're friends. Sometimes a defense lawyer has to be really mean and abrasive, and I don't want to be that way with you. I like you too much."

Meredith shook her head. "Scott, I had nothing to do with any of this. I want you."

Scott sighed. When he looked at Meredith, she knew she had him.

"Have you made any money off of the book? It certainly looks like you should have."

She shook her head. "They gave me a nice advance, but I used it to pay off some debt. The store's doing great, but the royalty checks won't be here for a while, so I hear."

Scratching his short beard with one hand, Scott tapped a pencil in his other as he looked at her.

She could tell he knew there was more to the story. But she wouldn't tell. She couldn't.

"Meredith, this is going to cost an insane amount of money. Insane. I hate to tell you how much I think it will be."

She closed her eyes. "Seven figures?"

"You're in the ballpark. I think it could realistically cost a couple million bucks. We need jury consultants and a team of investigators and God knows what else. I would basically quit doing any other case until it wraps up. And it's going to be a tough case to win. I mean, there's a map to the body in *your* book."

"I know," she said. "But if I'm going to spend my money on lawyers,

I would rather give it to you than anyone else."

"Well, we can start with a smaller number. But we're going to need some money."

"I know where I can get the money."

# Chapter 50

Her call with Allen wasn't pleasant. First, her friends had told her they felt she should have seen significant royalty checks by now, especially with the book being out for several months. Every time she brought the subject up to Allen he talked about reserves and foreign royalty reporting and made it seem like this was a normal schedule. Allen told her he would have to see if they could advance the money she needed; but that was highly unusual. He seemed off his game altogether. He wired the money she requested, based on a deal for her next novel as well as royalties from *Red Ribbon*, but he complained the entire time.

Two weeks later, Meredith still hadn't been officially charged. She wondered if she had been hasty in agreeing to another book deal, one that would provide her a two-million-dollar advance for writing two additional books. It was the latest in a long line of moments that should have elated her. It didn't. It filled her with dread. Her mornings now started at six o'clock sharp, when her body's urge to vomit woke her up, and she ran to the bathroom and wretched so violently she wondered if the neighbors could hear. She hoped they couldn't, but she didn't know if it mattered. They were too busy avoiding her altogether.

When she made her first trip to the grocery store and saw her face on a tabloid cover, she thought about loading up on some vodka and pills and cashing in. Or maybe she should hang herself from one of the River Street bridges. The people wanted a show, and how could she deny them? But she didn't have the courage, and besides, she hadn't actually killed anyone. She would have to live with a litany of sins to atone for; she had slept with the devil and given him everything. He held her life in his hands now. He had since the moment she sent him her feeble attempt at writing a novel.

Fame to infamy in a matter of months. She had assumed the one bright side of the press would be plenty of additional sales, but the opposite happened. The book spiked and then left the top twenty altogether. The commentators throughout the blogosphere went dark. The idea of writing a book to hide a map leading to a real body apparently proved too much for anyone to handle.

Bethany Lopez wrote an excoriating piece about her unease in her interview with Meredith, which couldn't have been more untrue. They had hit it off like best friends. Nate stood loyally by her side, Terrie and Jennifer came by as often as they could, and Lisa brought her a meal once or twice a month, but everyone else stayed away. Even Michael had deserted her. No email, visit, or phone call in more than a month.

The store felt like a ghost town. She could handle it for right now, but she knew before long, especially after a slow Christmas season, she would have to lay someone off.

Book dealers started sending requests for special inscriptions, ones they knew she couldn't write. One offered $5,000 if she would write "I did it" on the title page. Others were even more descriptive.

Looking back on it, even though she didn't want to be charged with anything, she could rest assured knowing she asked for the advance and signed the contract when she did. She didn't know if they would have given her the money if she had waited. She assumed they regretted their decision.

Scott was not a publicity hound, and he encouraged her to keep as low a profile as possible. He kept in daily contact, which she enjoyed, but his messages were getting dire. He was negotiating bond terms for her in case the district attorney did file, which would allow her to stay out of jail while awaiting the trial. She knew she would face the charges eventually. Then everything would be restricted, especially her travel, which she found the toughest thing to handle. She felt sure her house would sell immediately, given its placement and all the notoriety, but just like her book sales, the opposite held true. Scott told her that might not be the worst thing, as she could put it up in lieu of cash for a bond. She had been staying at the DeSoto, but he encouraged her to move back to her place, not knowing what that meant. He gave her strict instructions to only answer questions he asked. He sent out some investigators to uncover any possible angle, but her secret still hung around her ankle like a millstone.

Scott told her if they called before Christmas, it would be good news, as even the justice system liked to deliver the rare messages of hope before the holidays. No call came. When Scott called on December 28, Meredith braced herself for the words she expected to hear. Still, she couldn't breathe when, in a clear, kind voice, he said, "First-degree murder."

# CHAPTER 51

The first few days after being charged with murder were like being wrapped in gauze. Her doctor prescribed her some Xanax, which became her good friend. It gave her the ability to think when she needed to and not think the rest of the time. On the rare occasions her friends visited, she couldn't ignore their obvious discomfort. On the one hand, this made sense. She had been charged with murder, after all. On the other hand, she expected more from her lifelong "friends," including sticking by her in good times and bad.

Her return to the house made her doubly uneasy. Every room held a memory of her and Michael—his raving over her cooking at the dinner table; long, wine-driven conversations under the steady drone of the porch fan; nights of unspeakable passion in her bedroom, where the ghosts still blushed. And now she understood, what should have been an easily-seen manipulation, Michael pulled the strings of the ultimate wannabe—her—so sick to be a writer she gave up all reason and control over her life.

There were times when she could almost live with the idea of the lie if it just hadn't ended and she could have been left in the dark, continuing on with the lovemaking and the heady promises. She missed the physical side of their relationship. No one had ever touched her like he had. She thought about abandoning Savannah and finding a new man, a new life. She had no idea who would be her target, but it sounded like such a release to wind up in someone's arms. Someone who would stroke her hair and tell her it would be okay. She thought about it more than she cared to admit, as a distraction, as a comfort, and to reignite those insane and powerful nights. To have the passion wrenched from her hands felt like yet another injustice, another side of life Michael had supplied that no one else could.

She laughed as she realized she sounded like the narrator at the end of their novel. No place gave her more solace than the streets of downtown Savannah, which equally weighed heavy with sadness and promise. Legally, the pre-trial agreement meant she couldn't leave town until the trial, and truthfully, she didn't want to.

Although Scott was frustrated—he knew she wasn't telling him something—he always ended their meetings with a pat on the shoulder and a positive *keep at 'em* speech. It killed her not to tell. She knew it made no sense. But she couldn't.

Part of her defense was simple: other than her one trip, she had never been to The Shoals. Even during the one trip, she hadn't even come close to approaching the spot where the body was buried.

Trial or not, she was determined to prove she was an author—even without Michael Black. During her year in Michael's shadow, she had studied the form of the novel and demystified the writing process. Whether or not she wanted to admit it, he made her better. His emails stung more than she wanted to admit. He opened her up to listening to people differently, to realizing the sacrifices one made to a manuscript.

Dammit, she could do this. Without him. To all the doubters, including Michael—especially Michael—she would prove them all wrong.

# CHAPTER 52

The cameras didn't stay all the time; the neighborhood watch committee made sure of it. Her neighbors may have glared at her every time she went outside or, worse yet, completely ignored her, but they did serve their purpose. But the journalists wouldn't give up. They hid behind trashcans and disguised themselves as cable repairmen or delivery drivers. Meredith thought about giving them something to talk about, but Scott's voice would always appear in the back of her mind, warning her to keep a low profile. Unfortunately for the camera crews, her life was rather boring—other than the whole being charged with murder part.

She tried again to write. There were plenty of examples of great works of literature coming out of bad situations. Everything from *Don Quixote* to the inspiration for some of Dostoevsky's best writing. She developed a routine. Every afternoon at two o'clock, she opened her laptop and stared at the screen. It stared back. She once had an idea for a novel; it became a bestseller. Now, all bets were off. She tried to start again without having any idea in what direction she should move. She tried character sketches and old plots she had worked with before. She did this for weeks before realizing she was making things worse. She decided to return to the idea she had abandoned and make 2 p.m. her nap time instead.

Meredith learned even more to compartmentalize. She broke her life into breadcrumbs and celebrated completing each one. Brewing coffee. Making lunch. Going to the market. Taking a bath.

She still hadn't heard anything from Michael.

She met regularly with Scott. He had scheduled the trial for early August, which seemed like an eternity away, but he assured her it was almost too soon. Every conversation started with some variation of, "Is there anything else you need to tell me?" and Meredith making what she hoped was a sufficient amount of eye contact before changing the subject.

Her mind dwelled on prison. The bars, the cells, the loss of freedom. Meredith wanted to win the trial on her own merits. She wondered whether Michael would intervene, but she knew she couldn't count on it. She wasn't even sure he was still alive. She needed to distance herself from the physical evidence, which is what she kept directing Scott towards. She wanted to stand on her own feet with this defense.

She thought back to her quiet, serene life before Michael Black and her "dreams" came calling. She could tell the farfetched story of a man living in her garage, hope to be believed, and then go slip away. But then she would be known as a liar, too. She had a plan and would stick to it: state she was innocent of murder.

She couldn't tell her attorney what he needed to know, what would take his defense in a completely different direction. She tried to tell herself all of this was normal. She knew it was not.

# CHAPTER 53

Scott Pettit was a good lawyer. It didn't take him long to know Meredith hid something from him. Usually, his clients couldn't bear to say the bad things they'd done out loud. But this felt different.

Meredith had things going for her, and fame could help, but in her case, not much. She hadn't been famous long enough. He worried most about her attractiveness. Juries, especially female jurors, tended to dislike successful, beautiful women. He needed something concrete to put this case over the top and away from conviction altogether. His bets were on Michael Black. The prosecution floated the theory she and Michael had an affair and she envied and resented his new flame. This seemed like a plausible assumption. But why have the map in the book? Nothing about Meredith indicated she was diabolical enough to even conceive of such a thing. Everything Scott knew pointed to Michael Black. He just had no way to prove it.

He had his hands full with the prosecutor, Amanda Meadows. A great trial lawyer, she was considered a serious player in future Georgia elections. Sometimes, those two things were mutually exclusive. Not so with Amanda. Scott liked working with her, and while she seemed to return the favor, he also knew she had a few battle scars. Recently, he had won two high-profile abuse cases against Amanda; the press had scolded her for taking on too high of a caseload, something Scott told her in so many words before the cases even began. Savannah was a big enough city that it mattered, certainly in Georgia and, to a lesser extent, nationally, and she needed the next showdown to be a win. Scott refused to speak with deputy prosecutors about anything but the most ministerial things—instead, he wanted to hammer this out with Amanda, and she gladly obliged, sure she had a winner.

After court, they walked to Savannah Coffee Roasters near the Chatham County Courthouse. Anyone who saw them, knew what they discussed. Like Scott, Amanda only had this case on her plate. And every time she saw him, she wore the same cocky smile.

"She doesn't have a motive, Amanda," Scott said for the umpteenth time.

"Last time I checked, I don't have to prove motive," Amanda said, although they both knew she wanted to be able to do so. "I'll take a map to the murder scene in the book written by the defendant over any motive in the world."

Scott had to stare her down. This was obviously the case's weakest point and too glaring for him to evade. He needed Michael Black to go down to keep his client up. And considering the man's creepy reputation, it wouldn't be difficult to peg it on him—if he could find him.

"Look, Scott," Amanda said, "we know it's not your gal. I mean, a few people have a hard on for her, but most of us know. But for the life of me, I can't figure out why you aren't coming to me and using the obvious knowledge to help us send the real murderer up the river."

She read his mind. But Meredith hadn't caved and, apparently, never would. Scott hoped early on Amanda would see the holes in her side of the case and agree not to file until more evidence came in. He couldn't blame her for moving full-speed ahead; it's what he would have done if he were in her shoes. If he couldn't prove Michael Black's involvement, he knew Meredith's days of freedom were likely coming to an end. She would have to write her sequel from jail.

# CHAPTER 54

He hadn't intended this. That's what he told himself. But of course, he had intended it to be exactly like this. Even a sympathetic woman like Meredith couldn't stand to have his stench around for too long. She figured it out; he knew she would. And she cut him loose like anyone with half a brain would have done.

It was his third night sleeping under the floorboards of a stewardess's house in Gadsden, Alabama. She smiled at him in the airport lounge, and it was on—skip traces, Google searches, and finally a residence that could only be reached by going into the basement and up and through the subfloor.

Michael loved the feeling of near-suffocation. It was the sexiest hiding place yet. Lurking below her bathroom, he got to watch the woman put on a show. He could smell her and watch her shower, pluck her eyebrows, and pee and wipe. He wasn't supposed to be doing this. She hadn't given him permission—and it made it much better than rutting around inside of her.

Unfortunately, this target didn't move him in the way Meredith did. This gal had big titties, and that was about it. She also shaved her pubic hair down to a Hitler mustache, which he didn't like. He likely wouldn't have picked up on her at all, but he needed to take his mind off

Meredith.

Meredith left him. She feared him less than he thought she would be. She even seemed ambivalent about losing her fame, which he didn't expect. He had devised his plot so she would understand she was completely at his mercy. A velvet prison, the very best kind. She didn't understand she wasn't her own anymore. Not since she let him work and slave for hours, days, and months, polishing her manuscript to a shine.

She couldn't write, so to speak, to save her life. He had to give her some kudos on her storytelling skills, but damn, part of what attracted him to the manuscript was the sheer challenge of it. She thanked him, but it wasn't enough. She didn't understand all he had done for her. He would make her see it.

One day, Miss Meredith would be chained to a radiator, naked, having to give him the type of thanks he deserved. He would give her bread and water and wait until she got it right. Ungrateful bitch.

He didn't know if she realized he was BlackPlague. He figured she did, but it never came up in conversation. He had waited. He wanted someone else to find the clue, one so simple she should have never left The Shoals without deciphering it. He waited longer than he wanted. Nobody noticed. So finally, BlackPlague, who never had a nice thing to say about Michael Black, had to. It was a little obvious, he knew, but such was life.

He thought about pulling more stunts like the lipstick on the mirror but decided being hidden and silent terrified her just as much as his tricks—hence, his residency in Gadsden.

When Meredith first learned of his hiding place, he actually stayed around Savannah for a while, giving her a chance to repent and beg him to return. Then she sent the secret-keeping email, and Michael realized it would take longer to achieve his plan than he had originally anticipated. He found these stunning arched entry cotton warehouses right by River Street. They were clearly as old as Savannah itself, and they were perfect.

The road ran above them, making them sturdy and loud, and they were much bigger than the carriage house—the perfect hideout. Michael found, although they were supposed to patrol the area, the officers didn't like going in the rooms because someone like him could be hiding there. He only stayed there for a few nights, and he loved the feeling of being out in the open, waiting for someone to challenge him and living among the Savannah ghosts.

Michael was a patient man. He would wait for her. Gadsden suited him for now, but he would soon be heading back to Meredith. He was working on the manuscript he knew she would need.

# CHAPTER 55

Law Office of Scott R. Pettit
Savannah, GA

July 7, 2016

Ms. Meredith Harper
Via Courier

Dear Meredith:

I am sorry if I was short with you during our conference last Friday. I am frustrated, and I think it's time I lay it all out.

As you well know, we now stand just over four weeks from trial. I have a team of legal professionals working on your case from every angle. They are doing their best to find out what they can about the corpse—if it had been moved, how those old documents discovered in the kitchen are involved, the few other anomalies, and anything that could possibly exonerate you.

There are indications someone moved the body, which would help your case, but they are far from conclusive. Considering *your* book contains a map to the body, it's hard to ignore your involvement.

I understand your contention Mr. Black read the manuscript years ago. I have put most everything in place to show University Press did receive and process the work. However, since they did not publish it, they did not keep a copy of the manuscript, and everyone who actually worked there has retired or moved on. Those at the Press mentioned Black's recommendation extensively, but they never received it. I have to say this still leaves quite a conspiracy to put in front of a jury. There's no promise they will follow you and pin the crime on a man who hasn't been seen for a number of years.

I have to document that I continue to ask you for whatever piece of information you haven't yet given me, and you continue to change the subject every time I ask. I believe you are innocent; unfortunately, I also believe you are hiding something significant.

The entire legal community and I believe Michael Black is the killer. His relationship with Quinn gives him the motive you lack. I cannot imagine why you would hold something back that could keep you out of prison.

Please realize I am bound by strict rules of confidentiality, and I am proud to say I have never violated my oath. I would be happy to keep whatever information you have between us; however, even just knowing it would help me open up additional leads and possibilities.

Obviously, I haven't written a famous book and don't begin to understand what's going on in your head. However, having been in the innards of many Georgia prisons, I can tell you whatever you are hiding is not worth a prison sentence.

Let me help you.

Yours truly,
Scott
SRP/tp

# CHAPTER 56

Silence. The silence most unnerved her. He had begun to pop up more and more in her thoughts, and there were times she swore she could smell him. Especially in her bedroom.

The silence greeted her when she turned the lock on the back door. It accentuated the loss of her lover and reminded her of the dread she felt every night when she suspected he had returned. Most of all, it reminded her *she* had chosen to live without him.

*Why can't I let the lie go?*

But the deafening silence made it hard to think of any answers.

If someone didn't intervene before the trial started, she would get up on the stand and tell the truth—the whole truth and nothing but the truth. Surely, coming clean would be better than going to jail. But a part of her didn't believe she would go through with it. She asked God for forgiveness. Silence greeted her there, too.

She tried to cover up the hole he left in her life with things reminiscent of happier times. She played music loudly and combed through boxes of pictures, looking at herself with Terrie, Jennifer, and Lisa in odd hairstyles and Benetton Colors.

Where was that girl who walked beside them? The one with the gleam in her eye. Oh, to regain her old life. She was accused of murdering an innocent young girl whose only crime was loving the same deranged man. Somehow, she preferred being labelled a murderer to being seen for what she really was—a liar and a fake.

She felt thankful for the long, thick summer evenings, for the mosquitoes, for anything keeping the darkness and silence at bay. Once the sun finally took its nightly bow, she succumbed to Michael's clutches.

How could she miss his physical presence so strongly and be so terrified of him? She knew Michael was poison. But there were times when she would have given anything for his touch, for the danger lurking below the surface.

When sleep failed her, the real Michael showed up. The dream interrupter. The blood stalker. He hid behind every door and could reappear at any moment. Even if she never saw him again, waiting for him would always be part of her daily ritual, part of the prison she rebuilt every single day.

Perhaps the prison of fear and anxiety she had created was worse than the real thing. Maybe she'd finally be safe in prison.

Suddenly, Meredith heard a chair slide and squeak on the hardwood floor downstairs. She was sure of it. She moved to her bedroom door, inching it open as she listened. She had left the gun Lisa had bought her in a kitchen drawer downstairs. If Michael were down there, he would find it before her.

When no other sounds came, she relaxed, realizing it was another false alarm.

She didn't sleep for a long time.

# CHAPTER 57

Time inched by. Meredith's dreams came in funky Technicolor that night, filled with the stuff of nightmares, each barely occupying a sliver of the blackness. The dreams were always so similar. She always dreamed of Michael.

Suddenly, she woke up with a start. Standing over her loomed a dark figure. It smelled like him.

Her thoughts came slow and stuttering as she struggled to break free of her dream. She recalled the scene from *Red Ribbon* when Leah danced with the knife around the bedroom. Meredith couldn't make out Michael's face, but she didn't need any more information than his smell—a mixture of sharp cologne, sweat, and a hint of cloves, a scent she would always associate with him. It turned her stomach when it came back to her now, but sometimes when she lay in bed alone and horny, all she could think of was the way he smelled.

She rolled onto her side with her eyes shut, feigning sleep. Then a terrifying thought hit her. She *had* been smelling him. He'd been creeping in at night, watching her, checking up on her, and entering her dreams.

Meredith lay there, acutely awake, doing what she did best: pretending. She pretended she was a famous author. She pretended she wrote *Red Ribbon*. She pretended she didn't know anything else to help her case. And she pretended she never met Michael. Within a year, her entire life had become one big lie, and the second she started choosing what to finally tell the truth about, she knew her entire world would crumble like a flimsy house of cards.

Michael sat there for what felt like hours, his unwavering attention focused on her. She could feel his gaze on her skin like a chemical burn.

He reached for her hair and stroked it.

She tried with everything she had not to wretch. Michael had broken her. He would decide her future whether she liked it or not, all because of her unrelenting ego.

Finally, he eased off the foot of her bed and left her in her terror.

# CHAPTER 58

That night, Meredith couldn't fall back asleep. She stared at the ceiling, worrying he would return—or still watched her, hidden in the shadows. She didn't think he would kill her, but she feared he would pull her completely away from her moorings, leaving her more adrift and even more alone.

Perhaps more than anything else, the most disquieting thing was the past year and a half hadn't made her hate him. Instead, she found herself still considering what he would think and how he touched her—that scared her more than anything. She could no longer trust herself.

She needed to reclaim everything she'd lost. She needed to find herself again.

In the morning, Meredith reserved a room at the DeSoto. She wasn't ever going to spend another night in her house. Then she called Scott shortly thereafter and told him she wanted to meet late that afternoon. She had something to tell him. The truth. But first, she needed to go to Tybee.

Tybee Island was synonymous with Savannah. Just south of the city, many Southeasterners seeking a beach, without having to board a plane, vacationed there.

When Meredith was little, Tybee was the perfect, cozy beach spot and had much less of a party reputation than Savannah. Some of Meredith's fondest memories were of the tiny, permanent carnival spot, which had tiny rides for the smallest of adventure seekers. The place lit the night up in a neon glow. Miraculously, Tybee managed to hold on to its vintage charm. Although the arcade had disappeared, the streets were still lined with five and dimes, surf shops, and classic southern eateries.

She hadn't come to Tybee since the news broke, afraid of being noticed. Today, she didn't care. She would hold her head up high. Screw her reputation.

Hopefully, the sun's warm beams and the breeze's gentle caress would ease her mind. She scanned the crowd once more to make sure he hadn't followed her. She would erase him from her life.

She reached the large public pavilion near all the shops and restaurants, ordered a Corona from the beer stand, and sat in the shade. People swarmed around her. She saw sunburns and leathery skin and warring Alabama and Georgia football gear. She picked up her tote and walked down the pavilion to the long, low tide stretch of sand. She kicked off her flip-flops, and the feel of the sand on her toes brought her home. Home to before Michael, before she became famous and then infamous. She closed her eyes and felt the power begin to swell. Then she felt him. Like an unnamed narrator searching through the past, all of her synapses fired warnings. She snapped her eyes back open.

He had dyed his hair a ridiculous sandy blond color, and he stood there with a black Nike cap and a bare chest. He still had a strange tattoo of a falcon on his left shoulder. Their eyes met. His eye contact was brief but deadly. He wanted her to know he followed here.

Her legs were numb, her palms sweaty. Seeing him brought it all back: the feelings of love and admiration, the pride of having the artist you respect more than any share your bed and your life, the revulsion at the moment of pulling back those boxes and revealing him, dead to the world, choosing a desolate spot over her own bed. The threats, the flowers, the midnight visits. When she turned back, he had disappeared.

Meredith could hear her heart pumping. Since she was surrounded by people, she didn't worry he would kidnap her. She feared he would try to follow her to her new spot—or he might leave her forever.

She needed a buffer. She surveyed the crowd, and her eyes rested on a good-looking younger man speaking with a woman on the boardwalk. His muscles bulged out of his tank top. Perfect.

She walked across the pavilion and tapped him on the arm. "Excuse me." Her expectant eyes upon him.

He hesitated for a second and then said, rather too formally, "How can I help you?"

"I think my crazy ex is between here and my car," she said. "If he's here, it's not to enjoy the beach." She started to say more, but one look at him told her she had already said enough. "If you wouldn't mind, could you walk me to my car?" She made eye contact with the kid's female interest to make sure she knew she wasn't moving in on her man.

The girl nodded her approval.

The chivalrous gentleman assumed his role as protector. He clinched his teeth and asked, "How do you want me to handle this?"

Meredith tried to calm herself. "I don't think he'll do anything if you're here."

"Is he a problem?"

"Always."

When they reached the car, she didn't see Michael anywhere in sight. She edged closer to it, her southern hunk walking right along with her and his lady friend tailing behind. She peered through the front window. Sitting on the center console, a DVD rested in a sleeve.

"Everything okay?" her companion asked.

"Yes, he must have left. Thank you so much for your help."

Michael knew she wanted to take back some control over her life, but he put her in her place—again. She finally summoned up the courage to open her door, half-afraid he booby-trapped it. She quickly picked up the disc and turned it over.

The label read, *CONFESSION OF MICHAEL BLACK.*

# PART III
# HELL

"Writing is nothing more than a guided dream."

—Jorge Luis Borges

# Chapter 59

Meredith made a bee-line to the TV upon arriving home. After a scratchy transition, there he sat—Michael in front of a white board.

"I am Michael Black," he said, as if anyone had a doubt. "I wrote several books, and then, about six years ago, I disappeared." He held up a newspaper from last week to prove the video was current.

"I first read Meredith Harper's manuscript, *Red Ribbon*, several years back. She sent it to me in the hope I would blurb it. That was maybe eighteen months before I met Quinn Yancey.

"It has come to my attention Ms. Harper has been charged with the crime of murder for the death of Miss Yancey. That is impossible. I saw Quinn Yancey take her own life five years ago. She did it in a fit of rage and anxiety, and the physical evidence will bear that out.

"I panicked when I saw her kill herself. It ate me up. I knew I should have reported the death to the police, but everyone already hated me for having a relationship with such a young woman, and I figured they would pin the death on me. I buried the body, and by putting it in *Red Ribbon*, I made sure I had a way to find it if I ever needed to. I didn't know her book would ever see the light of day."

He couldn't help but put a dig in—even in his confession.

"The gun can be found at the Harbeson National Bank in Charleston. It is the weapon Quinn Yancey used to kill herself."

Meredith felt tempted to go and check this out, but she thought it best to leave it to the cops; plus, she didn't want to be anywhere near the evidence.

"I moved the body from Atlanta to The Shoals. The exact location of the actual suicide is also contained in the safety deposit box, noted in GPS coordinates. I am truly sorry for any trouble I have caused the Yancey family or anyone else, but it is completely unfair to charge Meredith Harper with this crime."

Meredith called Scott and told him she would be stopping by a little sooner than she promised.

On her way to his office, Meredith had a jump in her step as she realized maybe she could work this all out without having to humiliate herself. That sounded oh-so appealing. Then an idea came to her; her heart stopped. *What now*? Michael wouldn't confess to any crime just to set her free; he had something new in mind. She froze in the middle of the street and almost turned around. But she had been waiting for this. Whatever he did have in store, it couldn't be worse than life in prison. She kept moving, the spring in her step gone.

She showed Scott the video. She expected jubilation, but what she got was more nuanced. It would help, he told her, but why could she not have mentioned this before? Meredith, of course, had an answer for this, but she couldn't say it. She knew she could trust Scott, but now she had an out. And if her publisher liked her new novel, she could reclaim the fame she once had and move on from this hell. She had to keep quiet.

"You know, they're going to want you to help catch him," he said, as much to himself as to her.

"I have no idea where he is."

"They're not going to believe you."

Meredith smiled. "All I hope right now is they believe what's on the tape."

Scott nodded.

It was not as reassuring as she would have liked.

# CHAPTER 60

When Meredith got back to her house, she knew Michael had been there again. It made perfect sense, but it sickened her. She saw a letter on the table in Michael's handwriting.

> *M -*
>
> *I don't understand. It doesn't have to be this way. Yes, I was angry, and yes, you know you deserved it. But I'm taking care of it. Say you're mine, and let's go away forever. I have the plans. I'll wait for your answer online.*
>
> *- M*

The tone seemed wrong for Michael; college boy romance contrasted greatly with his usual cutting wit and visceral anger. Clearly, the angular handwriting belonged to him, and the breaking and entering was certainly his style, but something felt off. Was this a different tactic, or did he really miss her?

Despite what she still tried to believe, he didn't love her. He wasn't capable of love. Obsession maybe, but not love. His toying with her proved that. He could have confessed months ago, but he got off on watching her squirm.

She grabbed her purse and went to her car. She looked around for him, but she couldn't get herself to check the garage. She glanced under the SUV, sure a hand would reach out, and then climbed in. Meredith wasn't coming back.

# CHAPTER 61

Broderick had assumed Michael would emerge like this for months; he didn't go to the authorities because he thought more turmoil would have a greater chance of smoking him out of whatever hole he lived in. Amanda Meadows wouldn't sit back and let Michael go free. More than anything, he felt vindicated—for always believing Michael was alive and knowing once and for all he was involved in Quinn's death.

Meredith remained an enigma. Once she was charged with murder, why didn't she just give him over and end any chance she had of winding up in prison? The lengths people were willing to go to protect their own fiefdom. He despised the woman, but he did not believe she had harmed his daughter. Most likely, the charges against her would be dropped.

That didn't mean she was innocent. He just wasn't sure what she was guilty of.

The chatter between Michael and Meredith seemed to have ended. Broderick wondered if that would change now that Meredith was almost free.

# CHAPTER 62

It took Scott two more days—leaving Meredith to believe the trial would still go forward—but he finally struck a deal. Meredith would plead to one count of obstruction of justice. There would be no jail time to serve, and Meredith would have nothing but an ugly, meaningless spot on her record. At first, Meredith told him she would not plead to anything, but as the date of her inquisition drew nearer, Scott's persistence won her over. She didn't have children she would disappoint nor a crestfallen husband. Scott told her by amending the charges, they could never bring these issues up again, and that sounded heavenly.

Scott got Amanda to go so far as to open a courtroom early and have the plea done before the media caught wind. He wasn't perfectly pleased with this plea, but he had seen people convicted on far less in jury trials. His client would plead a murder charge into a no-fine, no-jail time misdemeanor. He would take that outcome any day.

The theory behind the plea agreement was Meredith had known Michael was alive and hadn't reported it. Since he had never been charged with any crime in connection with Quinn's disappearance, the conviction she agreed to take was based on very flimsy legal grounds. But it was better than a murder trial, as everyone assured her. She knew it would be front-page news all over the world. However, she could be long gone by the time they arrived.

She decided to get out of town and finish her novel. It had a great plot, very much in the spirit of *Red Ribbon*. Her agent liked the idea. He had worked to get the manuscript's delivery date pushed back to give her enough time to complete it. As soon as the plea was entered, Meredith would go to the airport and get on a private plane, which she had rented with the limited resources she had left. She would fly to Key West and spend the next weeks away from her Savannah life.

Nate, who she recently bumped up to a ten percent ownership in Southern Gothic, would run the store. She would dig herself out of this mess. She would bask in her next novel, cultivate it to its provenance, and be proud of the result of seeing her own words on the printed page.

The courtroom was a second-floor room not much bigger than a regular office. Scott told her they normally used it for divorce trials and probate disputes. A part of Meredith, as silly as it sounded, felt almost offended her high profile case ended up here and not in the grand courtroom it deserved. She checked herself. Good Lord, she pretended to write one book and had become an absolute diva.

She wore a boring navy suit she would jettison once on the plane. Scott stood with her. Amanda Meadows looked straight ahead at the judge as she read the amended charge. Some of Amanda's assistants, who watched half a year of their lives go down the drain, gave her death glares.

The judge who took the plea was stern and watchful and kept an eye towards the door in case the media should arrive. He frowned as Meredith droned the few words of her guilty plea to him. With that, she would not be tried for murder, and she could crawl back into respectable society.

She headed to Key West to write. And now, she could afford it again. Her royalty check had to arrive sometime. If not, Scott had handed her a small check of money he hadn't used the day before. It was just enough to give her the gift of time. These were good things.

Meredith had her freedom. She thought she would be celebrating like it was St. Patty's Day in Savannah. So why did the feeling of dread not leave her chest?

# Chapter 63

(Via email)

M-

Where are you? Where did you go?

-M

* * *

Warm, wild Key West.

She felt she'd aged a decade in the last year. She was free now. No bail, no lawyers, nothing but completing a book—a better one than *Red Ribbon*—and drinking margaritas. Most of all, she wanted to feel human again.

She rented a villa near the beach. Small and well-kept, it had a tiny backyard pool and vintage Cuban artwork—the kind of place she had always seen in *Beach Living* but never could afford. Now she could—she didn't think about how long it would take to see her royalty checks.

Meredith longed for a man, one who would make her forget she ever touched Michael Black. She hadn't been with anyone since Michael ripped the veils from her eyes and made her understand the expanse of human desire and how much physical pleasure another person could provide. She didn't need Michael's condescending emails about taking a lover. He didn't own her. Her own book would clearly outsell *Red Ribbon*, and she could forget him altogether. Who would believe him anyway? He was wanted for murder.

She took a deep breath and started making her masterpiece come together. It was hard work. She didn't want to be overly social until she did it. That attitude lasted until four o'clock the first afternoon.

Time for a drink.

* * *

(Via email)

My M-

I'm sorry if I offended you. I can't think of what it would be. I've always made sure you wouldn't be harmed. I FREED YOU! You must remember what you do to me. I need you back.

-M

# CHAPTER 64

Broderick could see the sonofabitch was decompensating. What the hell was he doing? Michael clearly had much better track of Meredith for the past year than he thought. He had all kinds of tabs on her, and now the filly decided to leave him hanging in the wind, and the little pantywaist's whole world went up in smoke.

The loss of control made Broderick very happy. Michael Black's discomfort made him even happier. But he enjoyed another side of the snooping even more–he liked watching Michael watch her. Eventually, the information would slip, and Broderick would be there to stick it in and break it off. He would make Michael wish he never laid eyes on his daughter. He hadn't decided if he would kill him yet. But he left it on the table as a potential option.

Now, with Michael coming apart at the seams, Broderick worried he was out of the loop as well. And while he would love to be following Meredith's every move, he believed Michael being out of sorts would eventually pay dividends. He put his fear of not getting the chance to greet Michael in person away. Still, he decided he needed more information. Staying ahead of the game wouldn't hurt. He needed information he could he get his hands on that Michael didn't have.

# CHAPTER 65

(Via email)

M -

Having trouble figuring this out. I MADE THEM cut you loose. At my potential expense. I made your troubles melt away, and now I can't even find you.

You could be going to jail if I hadn't stood up and saved your life. You OWE your life to me. I have been patient and kind and have given you the love and devotion your silly and ridiculous husband couldn't. My sperm work. Quinn taught me that. I gave you your life back, and you won't even THANK me for it?

I know now I gave up too much for Quinn. I should have crawled back into my four-poster bed with Kate. Been miserable. Raised those shitty kids and just kept on with things. But I wasn't strong enough. Quinn was young and vibrant, and you were married and not even pursuing me. I needed something other than a dried-up college sweetheart who couldn't even make a sound that didn't hurt my ears. How was I not going to fall for Quinn? She was beautiful, and she loved me.

When you get to middle age, you need excitement. Someone with an ass and a smile. Everybody needs that.

You weren't there. Yes, you reached out, but you weren't available.

If I could have met you then, I might have been saved. I wasn't a blood stalker yet. I promise.

You don't know, but I came to Savannah. I would follow you to work. Your husband was a bad boy and never drank the concoction I poured for him back then. When I came and saw you, it was like I didn't even exist. Then I saw those articles about your bookshop. You were supposed to be mine back then. You didn't even know.

Now I hunt. My prey is not beasts, but lovely ladies, the ones who spurn my advances. I haven't harmed any of them yet. That only happens if they turn up pregnant and refuse to shut up like Quinn. No, you're probably better to not give in to me.

For now, you're safe. But I'll find you.

I have a gift for you. You only need to say yes, and it's yours.

Answer me.

Talk to me.

I honor you.

-M

* * *

Two weeks later, even on a Monday, Key West still looked like a vacation brochure. High and clear, the bright blue sky lifted every mood. She felt her shoulders release a year's worth of tension as soon as she sipped her first local rum.

Every morning, before the crowds awoke, she rose early and went for a long walk down the beach. She would find an empty spot and sit, listening to the wind in the trees and the waves crashing on the shore.

She had found a calm that had eluded since her life went off the rails.

She sent the first draft of *Creeping Vines* to Allen with a hopeful note:

> Dear Allen:
>
> Hope all is well. I guess NYC is all it's cracked up to be since I can't ever pry you away. Here is my first pass at *Creeping Vines*. I think it has potential. Would love to hear your thoughts. Also, thanks for sticking with me through all of this. Michael has made all of this so excruciating. Thank you for being my friend and confidant.
>
> Back out to the Key West sun.
>
> Love you,
>
> Meredith

The response she got from Allen encouraged her, and he seemed to like what he had read so far. She only had two more weeks left to write in Key West but felt optimistic about finishing. She had grown as a writer, and the cloud cast over her by Mr. Black lifted. She hadn't checked her Hushmail account for almost a week. Those emails were so unpleasant and were beginning to make less sense. A pleading, rather than malevolent, tone colored the last one, and Meredith could sense Michael falling apart. Good. For everything he put her through, he deserved it.

But that was before she read the most recent one. Then all of her calm went out the window.

Before, she always assumed Michael had a definite method to his madness, and the genius remained as well as the devil. Now he was downright crazy.

She could see his smile, wherever he was, pleased he had blown her off her moorings. Pushing her, threatening her, owning her. That excited him. She could sense it now. He was a monster. She was done being nice.

Key West

Dear Michael:

Hi. Remember me?

I used to be your pupil.

Not so much anymore. Now I'm here in the sun, writing my own book. Allen loves it.

I've gotta go pretty soon because my daily lay will come by in a few minutes. I had to teach him some of your tricks, but he's a quick learner and has easily surpassed you. I see what you mean about the young ones—firm, tireless, eager, sexy.

Go find another girl to terrify.

Your former friend,

Meredith

As she went to hit send, she stopped herself. She would have a drink and let it marinate for a few minutes. It would make her feel good, yes, but come on. Was it smart? She downed her cocktail and quickly deleted the email. Playing with fire means you might be burned.

Mason worked at a neighborhood bar. He stopped by every afternoon. He had short, sandy hair and six-pack abs. He looked the part of Key West fling, and he could talk for just as long as she needed before she gave him orders and he enthusiastically obeyed. He generally went shirtless, which Meredith didn't mind one bit. One less thing to take off.

When he came by, the writing part of her day had finished. He was good to go for 90 minutes or so, and for the first time since all the madness, Meredith could completely let her guard down—along with her panties.

Meredith had lied when she compared him to Michael. Mason was a strong and satisfying lover but not wild like Michael. Meredith was convinced Michael tapped into his crazy when he made love. She doubted she would meet another one like him.

Her phone beeped with a new email.

> Meredith:
>
> The powers that be didn't like the new novel. At all. I asked them about the bones, and they said it had the bones of a meth user. Sorry. Just wanted you to know the tone of their conversation.
>
> They do not want to see this again. I say they may change their minds if we can make it more to their liking. They've extended the deadline (second time) to December 15 for your first draft submission. You have three months to make this work—should be enough, right?
>
> LK made it clear to me if she doesn't get it or doesn't like it, she's making a formal request for the return of the rest of the unsatisfied advance. At this point, when I calculate what you're still owed from Red Ribbon, it's a little over a million dollars.
>
> Sorry to ruin your vacation.
>
> Allen

Meredith held her head between her hands. She massaged her temples. She could do this. She looked at her watch. 1:30 p.m. Not long until Mason would make his shirtless appearance. She would let him make her forget—for at least 90 minutes.

# CHAPTER 66

How was she going to write a novel in less than three months? She thought *Creeping Vines* was pretty great. Maybe not better than *Red Ribbon* but equal. She wanted to blame it on her editor's bad taste, but she knew the truth: she wasn't Michael Black. In most ways, that was a gift from the heavens. At this moment, it felt like death.

He still wanted her. He begged for her to make contact. Would it be outrageous to ask him to write another book?

No. Michael was certifiable. She would tell the publisher she couldn't write another novel. She would pay them back from *Red Ribbon's* royalties or sales from the movie. Wouldn't that be preferable to speaking to that monster again?

He probably had other novels, she thought. He probably wrote one a year and left them in whatever hole he lived in. Proofread and copyedited little crystals of perfection—better than she could ever write with her sober, normal mind. It wouldn't be any sweat for him to give her one of those.

She looked up at the clock. 1:45 p.m. She let out a long and utterly pointless curse. She sat down at her computer. Maybe she should just check the Hushmail account again.

* * *

She couldn't do it. She couldn't make herself look at the email account. She told herself she didn't need to; deep yogic breathing and her daily visit from Mason would make it all better. When she saw Mason now, she felt guilty about bragging about him and how he didn't measure up to Michael.

But she liked this part of her life—being desired by a younger man, the certainty of the pleasure, the pure bliss of those island breezes with him next to her between the white sheets. In some ways, it reminded her of sending the first email to the Hushmail account, when she first asserted the smallest bit of independence.

Now she had changed her settings so she actually had to open the app to see her messages, which had calmed her. But not pressing the button left a loop in her brain that never closed; she knew she should be answering. But this was her working vacation, and she would enjoy it.

She looked at it as a victory. More distance from this devilish man.

# CHAPTER 67

(Via email)

Tuesday

Key West.

I knew you'd slip up.

I meant you could take a lover if I got to watch. Be involved somehow. Watch him deliver the goods so to speak.

I order you to stop seeing little Mason.

He will not like it if you disobey.

M

P.S. How do I know you're in Key West? Write to me, and I'll happily tell you.

* * *

Wednesday

M-

I notice you didn't even open your email yesterday. You are always good and prompt about that. I would hate to see Mason have to bear the burden of your mistake. I really don't hold any animosity toward him. He's a horny boy. In a way, we have that in common.

Take this seriously, Meredith. Talk to me. I am in control again.

Your blood stalker

* * *

Thursday

M-

Really? You've gone AWOL again. You don't even know I watched you two today. You don't know I have your panties sitting here next to me. You looked for them for a couple of minutes and then went into the bathroom.

Mason did a serviceable job. I'll give him some pointers at some point if he wants. But if you don't respond to me by noon tomorrow, he's not going to like me very much. He's going to blame me. But you're the one who holds the key to his ... completeness. Get my drift?

Too bad, so sad.

Your blood stalker.

* * *

On Friday, in her early afternoon time when she really did little more than think about Mason, she couldn't take it anymore. She decided to check the account to shake the strange feeling she had been having. She breathed deeply as she opened the emails.

Her heart sank as she read them. She looked at the clock—well after noon. *Oh God. What had she done? What would he do?*

She grabbed her phone and called Mason. Straight to voicemail. She called again, hoping he was just on the phone. Same thing. Kicked to a voicemail he hadn't even bothered to set up.

She tried one more time with the same result. Then she texted.

```
I think you may be in danger.
Is everything okay?
My ex may know about us
He is deranged
Psycho
Pick up ur phone!
Mason!
```

The read receipts said they were not being received.

She put down the phone and went to the front door, hoping she could see him, hoping he would come and would somehow still be okay. She went to the kitchen and poured herself a shot of whiskey and felt the burn as it screamed down her throat. Surely, that would calm her nerves. She stood there, half a room away, when she heard the sickening *plink* of her cell phone, telling her she had a new text message. She ran to the phone.

```
This isn't Mason. This is Michael. Mason's on his way. Check your email. The one you've been neglecting.
```

# CHAPTER 68

(Via Email)

M-

Okay. I'll tell ya. Spill my trade secrets. Saw you finally read these. Too little too late for poor Mason. If you care.

Silly girl. If you leave an email unsent but open for more than a minute, it creates a draft. Didn't you know? I'm as computer illiterate as they come (look at my manuscripts—hell, I might as well type the damn things on a typewriter), and I still know about autosave.

Mason lost a finger on his right hand for stealing my woman. Could have been avoided as you well know, but you can explain. After watching, I considered cutting off his penis. He came quite close to getting that treatment. Call me homophobic, but I couldn't. What I did to him? Sharp ax, foolproof clamp. It's a sure thing. I hope he hasn't lost too much blood. He screams, you know. Quite a lot. Maybe you like that. Today, though, I don't think he's going to be able to fuck you to your expectations. The only thing getting hard this afternoon is his frozen finger, packed on ice, en route to you.

I had to bribe someone in New York to get a copy of the novel. Really? You should have at least let me read it. It's not good. I doubt they'll like it at all. It reminds me of a novel a writer—one who seemingly hasn't learned much of anything—sent me once. I stand ready to write you a novel. All you have to do is ask. You don't even have to guess my name. I'll be your Rumpelstiltskin.

-M

* * *

She ran from the computer to the door and opened it to find Mason holding a zip-lock bag filled with ice and his bloody finger. His face held a look of betrayal and fear. He fell to his knees, holding the bag out to her.

She pulled out her cell, dialed 9-1-1, and then reached down to comfort him.

"Do not touch me, lady." Terror seeped through his words. He looked around, carefully. "Please, just leave me alone."

"This can't be happening," she said. "Mason, I'm going to get you help, okay? Everything is going to be okay." Who was she kidding? Anyone who ever got close to Michael Black was never okay.

"Your husband's crazy," he said, pushing her away. "He said to stay away from you and be thankful it wasn't worse."

"I'm sorry," she said, pleading with Mason's crumpled body. "I'm so, so sorry."

He passed out before the paramedics arrived.

She kept repeating "I'm sorry" like a mantra to no one in particular. They sounded hollow, of course.

# CHAPTER 69

(Via email)

Master:

I need your help. I know that now. I cannot do what you do.

I'm back in Savannah. I'm sure you know. I hope my return makes you happy.

I need a novel. I am begging. My due date is December 15. I cannot have another mistake like the last one.

I cannot be your lover ever again. I'm sorry, but I can't. But I can be your pupil.

Will you accept?

Pupil

* * *

Master:

I expected to hear from you by now. I need the manuscript in just over a month. I am a nervous wreck. I wish I weren't, but I am. Please write back.

Pupil

* * *

Broderick wanted to puke. This woman played right into Michael's fantasies. He read about the craziness in the Keys from the Hushmail account and, from a friend who lived down there, pieced together how Michael got away in a helicopter like a villain from a Bond movie. Michael had enough money and nothing to spend on it; he could have any situation rigged to his advantage.

He hated Meredith. What a simpering fool. She clearly couldn't write the back of a Corn Flakes box, much less a novel, but she lapped up being famous. Hell, from what he could tell, she didn't even have a lot of money, and that was part of her problem.

But he could see it coming. Michael would make her wait and beg until the very last minute at which point he would deliver another damn fine, twisted novel.

And then Broderick would have the best chance he would ever get to introduce Michael to the wonders of a dull blade and a car battery.

# CHAPTER 70

(Via email)

M-

Here is chapter one of what I have completed. You will have to come pick up the entire manuscript to read it.

-M

# CREEPING VINES

## CHAPTER ONE

Flickering red and orange light bathed Reverend Batchelor's face as he approached the pulpit. The September night had cooled, but a sheen of perspiration dotted his brow from the warmth of the fire. The congregation's faces shone in the firelight, but those in the far corners were masked in murky shadows where light lost the battle with darkness. Brimming to capacity, several stood outside the tabernacle, waiting to be blessed by his every word.

A thrill of breathless excitement ran through the crowd when he gripped the sides of the podium. His might be the fifth sermon of the day, but by God, his would be the best. The camp meeting had brought dozens of self-styled preachers to the campground, each sure they were the next Jonathan Edwards. While they knew the Word of the Lord, they lacked what the Reverend Batchelor had honed to perfection—the ability to hold the congregation in the palm of his hand.

He'd made sure the fire had been stoked prior to his entrance so his shadow would loom large on the wooden backdrop behind, echoing his every movement, making him larger than life. He took a moment to scan the crowd; men and women from all stations of life filled the rude wooden benches along with their children, while the slaves of the wealthy huddled in the back. All waited eagerly for him to begin. His powerful glare alone could convert unbelievers.

He straightened and pitched his voice to the heavens. "You are condemned to Hell."

Reverend Batchelor paused until the last echo of his thundering voice had left the tent. Leaning forward, he scrutinized a scruffy-looking lad in the second row.

The boy trembled.

He softened his voice and spoke in a fatherly manner. "You are a sinner, a rebel against God and the wages of your sin is death." He lowered his head in sorrow. "You cannot enter the gates of Heaven."

His target gripped the roughly-hewn bench so tight his knuckles turned white.

Reverend Batchelor nodded as his gaze swept the crowd; their eyes widened, and their mouths gaped. He thrust his arm in the air. "Not unless you confess your sins and change your heart."

The congregation jumped when the fire popped, sending a burning coal skittering across the dirt to smolder at the feet of those in the front row.

Prowling across the stage, Reverend Batchelor used the theatrics God had provided. "Satan owns your soul and unless you seek forgiveness from your merciful Father—" He pointed to the fire. "You will roast in the fires of Hell for all eternity."

Time to let the whiskey makers and whores hiding deep in the surrounding woods hear his voice. "You must fall on your knees and bare your soul, laying everything before the Lord to escape this dire fate. Let God's Word scour and cleanse you. Let Him save you from Satan's scourge."

He thumped the pulpit. "Cast aside the desires of the flesh and allow the Holy Spirit to fill you."

Reverend Batchelor opened his arms as if to embrace the congregation. "I beseech you; turn away from Satan and beg the Lord, your Divine Heavenly Father, for His forgiveness."

He stepped from behind the podium and stared through the curling smoke from the edge of the stage. "With every eye closed, every heart open, I ask you, the sinner, the backslider, and even the highest deacon of the church, to come forward and kneel in the dust before me. I ask you to acknowledge your sins and to be judged by an angry God. Confess and feel the relief of a soul set free."

The scruffy lad from the second row bolted to the aisle.

"Brother Gribanow, please lead us in a hymn of salvation while I bless those sinners who have the courage to seek the forgiveness of their Father."

Because instruments enticed the devil, the drone of voices commenced, unaccompanied.

The believers filled the aisle as they made their way to the altar. Husbands. Wives. Weeping children. Slaves from the Negro section. The Reverend laid his hands on them, praying for their salvation. Each repentant still in command of their tongue murmured their thanks as they left.

A claw-like hand grasped his. "You are a messenger from the Lord, Reverend. May God bless and keep you."

The gnarled old woman before him smiled, face wreathed in wrinkles and back bent from hard labor. He peered over her shoulder and searched the crowd for the one face he desperately needed to see.

Reverend Batchelor placed his hand on the old woman's. "The spirit of the Lord lives strong in you, repent your sins and testify your salvation."

She bowed her head to pray, and he searched the crowd again.

There, between the second and third row of pews, stood Molly Hamilton, the desire of his heart. Their eyes met, and she looked away, a smile tugging at the corners of her lips. His heart raced at her display of bashfulness. Such a pure and innocent soul was indeed a rarity.

After the meeting, he would take her by the hand, and they would walk into the woods beyond where the whiskey mongers dared to venture. He would spread the blanket he had brought with him on the ground, and then the Reverend James Batchelor would take her innocence or take her life.

# CHAPTER 71

He had done it again. Taken her plot and turned it from straw into gold. She would make sure to get away from him this time. She accepted playing a certain role with him to get what she wanted, but she knew she could not find herself consumed again.

Meredith realized Michael needed to believe he had some control over her. He would allow her to sleep with a man provided he approved it. Disgusting and wrong, yes, but for now, she would do whatever it took.

She wrote him a short email telling him she loved the first chapter. She still had a week before her deadline. Surely, she would have plenty of time to study the manuscript and learn what turns the book would take and how closely it mirrored her outline. Maybe if she wanted to write another, she would suggest the arrangement they had created: she built the bones—*no longer of a meth user*—and he hung the flesh.

Her heart sunk when she received his reply an hour later.

* * *

My Dearest Pupil:

Your latest idea for a novel brings us into the territory of camp meetings. A great and utterly southern idea, one I am, frankly, sad I didn't think of first.

Therefore, I suggest we meet at Fountain Campground near Washington, Georgia at 6 p.m. on December 14. Fountain is one of the oldest camp meetings in Georgia. In the witchy part of winter, with no campers around and the sun closing up shop early, it is a still and dramatic place, filled with the atmosphere your readers have come to love.

I need time to finish some things, but it will feel good to be back in such a sacred place.

Come alone. I will as well.

Here's to solving problems.

Love,

M

* * *

She wanted to reply and tell him this was not acceptable. His email arrived the day before the manuscript was due, after all. But she knew she didn't dare.

# CHAPTER 72

When he saw the email, Broderick started the preparations. He pulled out the knives and scalpels he had collected. He would love to think he would have time to use thirty or forty knives on Michael, but he knew that was a pipe dream. He sharpened two of the knives and left one dull and rusty. He broke the top off of one of the scalpels in the hopes it would be more painful.

Then he kneeled in front of his utility room cabinet and removed "Sparky," the car battery he acquired just for this purpose. He held the cables together and heard a satisfying zap.

First, he would hit Michael with twenty cuts and flays, a minute between each one, enough to create anticipation and fear. Then he would go for Sparky, sending jolts to his nipples, genitals, and lower lip—once to each spot so he wouldn't go into shock. And then, if all went as planned, he would stuff Michael into a tiny closet, his underwear stuck in his mouth, leaving him to dread whatever came next.

Death would be too good for Michael Black.

Broderick felt ready. In his mind, he had practiced plunging the knife in a thousand times. He knew how it would feel.

He wanted his daughter and his life back. He could reclaim neither. He hated the pleasure he took in the preparations. But he hated Michael

Black more. Michael made him into this dark, brooding, killer. Michael had coaxed his ugly side to light. Michael sucked the love straight from his heart and left a mass of black lead in its place. Michael Black had killed more than just one person that night. He killed Broderick's grandchild, and he killed Broderick, too.

The toll had been tremendous. And it was finally time to make him pay.

# CHAPTER 73

It took three-hours to drive from Savannah to Augusta. The Augusta FedEx's last drop-off for overnight delivery was at 7:00 p.m., so she needed to leave the campground, manuscript in hand, by 6:15 p.m. Not much time to chat with Michael, thank God.

She didn't notice the Ford Ranger parked on the side of I-20 as she neared her exit. She did not see the man pick up the car jack he had placed beside the road for cover. Michael's hair hadn't changed since the beach—still blond and short—but with the beard he had grown, he looked different. He got in his truck and followed her.

Both cars passed the next exit. Neither of them saw a car on the overpass merge onto I-20 and also head west. The truck stayed behind both of the other cars but made sure to always keep the Ranger in sight.

A sliver of the moon cast a dim light in the dark night sky and over the quiet road. Worry gnawed at her. If anything went wrong tonight, she was far away from help. How stupid of her to agree to meet him out here all by herself.

When she finally saw a sign for the Fountain Campground, Meredith turned onto the dirt road. Utter darkness enveloped the car, and her headlights barely cut through the oppressive winter blackness. Three whitetail deer leaped in from of her car before disappearing into the woods. Meredith's heart thumped in her chest. The place was completely deserted.

She arrived at several cabins, the vapor lights dimly reflecting off their tin roofs, and parked her car. Meredith craned her neck to see if she could spot Michael. She opened the car door and walked out to stand in front of the cabins, sawdust softening her footfalls.

Michael could be hiding in any of the cabins. They all faced the tabernacle in the center. She looked at its silhouette and realized she couldn't see five feet past it. Its ancient pine benches could hold a thousand people if they needed to, but she doubted they saw crowds like that anymore. Nowadays, they were more often used for Boy Scout camps and family gatherings.

A pinecone fell and bounced off the tabernacle roof, startling her. She gripped the rape whistle hanging around her neck and put it to her lips. But it would do no good; there was no one else within miles except her enemy. She grasped the Taser she had brought a little tighter.

Meredith had been to camp meetings in southern Georgia and knew of their slow Southern rituals and smells of fried chicken and Brunswick stew. Now, on a dark winter night, the few vapor lights only seemed to highlight the darkness like a scene from another ghost story.

Another deer jumped from its hiding place and danced into the darkness, startling her again. The woods quickly ate the deer whole, and Meredith stood alone in silence again. Where was he? She checked her phone. No service. The time approached six. Of course, he would be late.

Meredith heard the car before she saw the headlights.

He drove twenty yards into the clearing, parked, and turned off his headlights.

He grinned from ear to ear.

Victorious, she supposed, having talked her into meeting out here in the middle of nowhere.

He walked toward her like a desperado in an old western, hands to his sides, a smirk on his face. He held the manuscript in one hand.

"My pupil," he quipped. "Why, you don't look a day older than when I saved you from a murder charge."

"I see you're just as charming as ever," she deadpanned.

"And I see you're still chasing your dream of actually being a writer someday."

Meredith steeled herself. *Stay cool, don't let him to get you.*

"And don't piss me off, or all of this writing could get scattered to the four corners of the forest," Michael continued.

Meredith walked towards him.

He moved back, dangling the manuscript above her head like a dog treat. "It didn't have to be like this," he said.

Meredith shook her head. "No, Michael. With you, it always would end up like this."

He moved a few steps away as if he were leaving. "So judgmental. So egotistical. So selfish. Fine, it looks like you don't need me. I'll see you around."

Meredith started after him. "No. Wait."

He turned dramatically and grinned. "Now … I think you should beg."

She bit her lip. Her eyes had adjusted to the light enough to see him.

They made eye contact.

"May I please have the manuscript?"

"Get down on your knees." He stretched the words.

She did as he said. She tried to breathe deeply. She prayed this would soon be over.

"No. Say please." He patted her on the head.

A whole ocean of sorrow rose in her. How had she ever loved this man?

He let her get up.

As she put her hands on the ground to get up, two years' worth of tears filled her eyes. She fought hard to fend them off. She did not want him to see her cry. "Please, Michael."

"See how easy it is when you behave?" He gave her the manuscript and beckoned her toward one of the overhead lights.

She flipped through to the first chapter to check it was the same novel. It included a cover letter he had written in her voice, and she read it hastily. Satisfied, she pulled the adhesive strip off the addressed envelope and sealed the package.

"I promise it'll be a best seller," he said.

She glared at him.

He grinned at her.

While she took the time to make sure everything looked correct, she couldn't help but smell the blend of cologne and bourbon she still found intoxicating—a dangerous combination of repulsion and desire.

Meredith turned back to her car, her heart beating in her chest, the envelope under her arm.

"Gotcha!" Michael yelled, and reached out to grab Meredith playfully.

Meredith's heart seized and she screamed. He scared her so much everything she was carrying, including the Taser, dropped to the ground.

Michael laughed wildly. "Had to have a little fun with you. For old times' sake, ya know?" He bent down to pick up the package she dropped. Then, like a deft Atlantic City magician, he quickly replaced it with one he had hidden in his coat.

Meredith, still recovering from the scare, missed his sleight of hand.

"Here you go." He looked her right in the eye as he straightened up and handed her the package. "I guess I'd better give you a chance to get to Augusta."

Broderick welcomed Michael's performance. While he focused on Meredith, Broderick crept up to Michael's Ranger and slipped a small radio transmitter under the back bumper. Then he snuck back to his vehicle, watched them get back into their cars, and drove away.

# CHAPTER 74

When she sped into the FedEx parking lot, the clock read one minute until 7:00. She leaped out of her car just as a sulky teenager in a blue and orange uniform put out his cigarette.

"Truck just left," the boy said while unwrapping a stick of gum. He pointed to a truck about to pull out into Augusta traffic.

Meredith ran to the truck, safety be damned. She found the angle most likely to catch the driver's eye and screamed so loudly the whole neighborhood must have heard. Meredith saw his brake lights come on.

"Please take this package," she shrieked, in a way more like a threat than a request.

The driver, who had probably experienced this before, didn't even try to protest. He simply pulled out his scanner and quickly entered the information.

She handed the package to him, written in Michael's handwriting and already marked for special early morning delivery, and sent it on its way. As she gave it to him, she realized she hadn't even kept a copy. Idiot. But at least her dreams were intact.

Being out in the forest with Michael had drained her. With her adrenalin spent, she longed for sleep. She found the nearest hotel, a surprisingly nice Doubletree, and checked in to a room with a king-sized bed.

Why hadn't she made a copy of the manuscript? How could she be so stupid? She had been a robot for the last month, and now she looked back on her actions, embarrassed. Really? She couldn't have asked them for another day? Her anxiety had drained her of her common sense, and now the rest of her brain could tell her how stupid she had been.

And despite everything he had done to her, she would still love to read another one of his books, and she would undoubtedly like it. It had been nearly a year since the discovery of Quinn's body. Maybe this new manuscript would put everything back together.

By the time she took a scalding hot shower, her vision began to return. Her heartbeat calmed, and she realized she had been in a panic—a pure terror had given her tunnel vision. In her desperation to fix her life, she had clouded her judgement and the ability to think rationally. She bit her lip and tasted blood.

How frantic and foolish she looked yet again. She drew the blackout blinds and climbed into the starched, white sheets. Sleep came quickly. A black, dreamless sleep.

# CHAPTER 75

Meredith slept for ten hours. When she woke from her coma-like state, she reached for her phone on the bedside table. Twelve missed calls. All from Allen. This couldn't be good.

She dialed him, and he picked up immediately.

"Thank God," he said. "You're okay." He exhaled like a nervous parent, his voice heavy with relief.

"I'm fine. Why do you ask?"

"Because of the book. Oh, and thanks, by the way, for sending it 1992 style in paper form with no disc. Break out the Day-Glo and turn up the Arrested Development.

"About that. I spilled coffee on my copy. Can you scan me one?"

"Well, that's how we had to deliver it to the publisher, so I guess we can do it for you," he said, still a little edge in his voice.

He normally didn't act this jolly. It seemed almost too much.

"What did you think?"

"Obviously, I haven't been able to read every page, but it's pretty great. Super ballsy. I've never heard of an author putting her own suicide in a book, though."

He continued talking, but she didn't hear the words.

"What?"

"And I just thought with the year you had, well, anything's possible."

Meredith felt dizzy. "I … I thought the book deserved it," she said, scrambling for words.

"Don't be modest. It's a pretty great scene."

She had to be careful here. She didn't want to give herself away. God, she hated having all of these things to watch.

"Murder-suicide, whatever you want to call it. The bastard finally getting what he deserves. I love that you put that in there."

Meredith needed to read the manuscript.

# CHAPTER 76

(Via email)

M-

Did you get a chance to read it yet?

Come back to Savannah, sweet. Let's be a literary Bonnie and Clyde. Or Romeo and Juliet.

I have it all planned out. If you can get me, you don't have to die. But it'll be more fun if we do it together. Your house, 4 p.m.?

Our secrets will go to the grave with us, and you will become a legend.

-M

* * *

Meredith had given Michael everything, so it shouldn't have surprised her he expected her to give him her life, too. She had traded the good for the perfect and given up her own life for a worthless immortality.

Michael hadn't treated her any differently than Quinn or Kate. He gutted her and threw her out like the trash. He made her dance and get naked and then ripped her apart, all to give him pleasure. She wasn't special. She was only a toy to him.

Meredith would be brave enough to own up to her crimes. She would tell the world and live in infamy. But she would *live*. She did not have to be a butterfly pinned in a frame.

She needed help. It was time to get the police involved.

She replied, short and sweet.

Clyde -

I'll be there.

- Bonnie

# Chapter 77

Michael didn't really think Meredith would give up and return to Savannah. Even his fantasies weren't so naïve. He would give her the benefit of the doubt, but if she failed him, he would end it.

His plan worked like this: if she went to Savannah, he would let her live. If she disobeyed him, she would die.

He waited forever for her to wake up and read the message. Her reply was tame; she would be returning to Savannah. That told Michael she would most likely not be returning to Savannah. He assumed his position at the periphery of the Doubletree, his binoculars trained on her room.

An hour later, when she walked out of the hotel into the orange sunlight, he felt the Viagra kick in. Her eyes were puffy, and she wasn't wearing makeup, but she still did it for him. She was still his forever girl. She wandered across the pavement tenderly, her head down, defeated. Maybe she really was going to Savannah. The thought made his blood stir. He loved the moment when they gave everything to him. When he had sucked them dry. She had given him everything but her life—at least, not yet. Oh, how he loved it.

He gave her fifty yards and pulled out onto the road behind her.

She merged onto the I-20 going west as if she were heading towards

Atlanta, away from Savannah. Although he had expected it, the choice infuriated him. He needed to stop her.

# CHAPTER 78

Broderick had his phone rigged so he would know as soon as Michael pulled out. It beeped and gave him an update. Not wanting to fall behind, he had chosen to nap in his truck.

He read the emails and decided he should wait in the car—wait for the opportune moment to act. He held back to see if she would be stupid yet again.

When he saw Michael heading west, he craned his neck around and saw Meredith ahead. She wasn't going back to Savannah. *Thank God*, he thought.

He pulled his truck back and let Michael have a little more rope. He was on the trail. When he saw her turn off in Thomson, he had a feeling he knew what was going on.

# CHAPTER 79

Meredith hadn't read a book in months. In the time leading up to the trial, she was too emotionally drained every night to keep her eyes open past eight o'clock. Then in Key West, she had a novel to write and Mason to enjoy.

She planned to find a hotel, alert the police, stand back, and let them catch the deranged man.

Thomson, a city close to Augusta and not far from Fountain, had a Hampton Inn, and seemed like the perfect hiding place for a day or two. She'd get settled in, call the cops, find a cheap novel, turn off her phone, and hibernate. Or perhaps by that time, Allen would send her Michael's manuscript so she could figure out what the hell he was talking about.

She pulled into the Hampton Inn's parking lot. She fiddled with her phone and checked to see if Allen had sent her anything. Nothing yet. She thought she had better check her email and see if Michael knew she wouldn't be attending his little party. For once, there were no emails there either.

A wave of paranoia hit her. She checked her surroundings, but there was no one who looked like Michael, just a spry older man walking quickly into the hotel. She looked again, just to make sure, and grabbed her bag out of the trunk and headed inside.

The clerk stood behind the front desk, a bored look on her face and gum popping in her mouth. The old man now sat in the lobby, scrolling through his phone.

Everything felt like a chore. She just wanted to climb back into bed.

"Have any rooms?"

"I have a bunch," the clerk said. "What do you want?"

"I just need a king bed."

The clerk started to mutter under her breath.

"Excuse me?" Meredith asked. She felt too exhausted to deal with this. Her whole body ached to get into bed.

"I said, that will be $210.25. Credit or debit? And I'll need to see an ID."

"Credit, thanks." Meredith handed her a card and her ID and waited.

"Okay. Room 233. Elevator's to the right. Continental Breakfast from six to ten."

The old man walked past her. He headed down the first floor hallway.

The clerk took forever, dropping the key and launching into a detailed explanation when she found it on the floor. Meredith really didn't care. She didn't want to be rude but just wanted her to make the damn key.

Finally, she made the key, still all thumbs, and handed it to her with a smile.

Meredith offered a fake "Thank you" and pivoted away as quickly as she could.

She rode the elevator up, walked all the way down the hall, and collapsed on the bed. Maybe she should extend her reservation and stay here a while. The anonymity, the thing she would have dreaded and ridiculed a year before, now seemed a sweet panacea for this never-ending nightmare.

Since she had been charged with murder, she rarely slept well. Instead, she rode an all-night coaster through the narrow zone between waking and resting. She could feel her subconscious pulling her back underneath, the *whoosh* of the heater lulling her into a tired purgatory.

Suddenly, she heard a *click*. She leaped out of bed. "Michael?"

She thought the sound came from the closet, but she couldn't bring herself to open the door. Oh God, not more nightmares. No more of anything. She walked slowly back and forth across the room, breathing deeply, the beat of her heart slowing. She didn't hear anything else.

She crawled back into bed, and her body pulled her mind back into a drowsy long hallway. Scenes flickered—Michael showing up on the porch for the first time, as if by magic out of the darkness, smiling at her, making her feel truly seen for the first time; the first rainy night with him, snuggling next to him, his arms wrapped around her, pulling her close.

Those memories shackled her; they would own her forever. Her breath caught in her chest for a moment, returning her to the waking surface. She pulled the sheets up over her head.

# Chapter 80

She heard another *click*—the sound of a key card in the lock and the handle turning slowly. She felt the steel fingers of fear run up her spine.

Michael grinned at her as he came through the door. "Chapter Eighty." He read from the papers in his hand. "Michael entered the room, knowing now the woman he had seen as his protégé and pupil was nothing more than a cheap whore."

Meredith looked around. It was too late to hide in the closet, and besides, she could only stay in there for so long. So she lay there, listening to the words wash over her.

He read on. "He wondered if she knew how much he loved her, how many nights he had hidden, protecting her from the rest of the world. He wondered if she would ever know."

Meredith opened and closed her eyes slowly several times. Yes, this was real.

"He decided to let her choose her method of death: slit of the wrists and watch her life float out like a crimson sea or a needle of heroin to her vein and let her soul rise with the stars and clouds. He asked her what her choice would be."

Meredith didn't respond—she had nothing left to say.

A look of frustration crossed Michael's face. "Meredith, what do you chose?"

She sat up, suddenly awake. "Michael, please," she said, in the sweetest and calmest voice she could muster, "it doesn't have to be this way. You know how much I love your books. How much I appreciate everything you've done for me. I would be no one without you. Michael, listen ..."

Michael sneered. "You aren't capable of love." He moved closer to her. "Now choose, or I will just start cutting until I get the desired result."

She thought back to her childhood prayers but couldn't remember anything. *Oh please, God, save me*, she thought. *Please save me from my own horrible, selfish choices.*

She looked at Michael, standing over her, daring her to resist. He had trapped her and destined her to die like Quinn at his hands—the hands of the man they both thought they loved.

"I want you to know one thing you've never asked. Don't know if you've figured it out. How did I know to get to Key West so quickly?"

Meredith hadn't even considered the question.

He continued. "Our little friend Allen—let's just say I played on a few weaknesses."

Meredith just stared, realizing how deep the deception ran. "Allen?"

Michael nodded. "My bitch. Sewn up tight. And with my employees at Gandolfo-Griffie, I didn't have any trouble keeping everything from you."

It hit her all at once. *His* employees? "You have a controlling interest in the company?"

Michael shrugged. "Something along those lines. When I got my last deal, I got a nice piece, and then I bought the rest. Hell, it's come in handy."

Then, like the final scene from a Michael Black novel, she noticed the mirrored closet inch open, and a face peered out. The man from the lobby. How could she not have realized it before? Quinn's father was the only man who hated Michael more than she did.

He motioned for her to stay silent.

She moved her eyes back to Michael, hoping he hadn't noticed her change in focus. If he had, he didn't let on; his eyes continued to bore into her.

Broderick Yancey crept out of the closet door, a bone-handled knife in his right hand.

"I reread *Cecelia* just recently," she cooed, trying to buy her savior time. "It's just so good. So mesmerizing." In her peripheral vision, she could see Quinn's father edging closer. He was now close enough to tackle Michael and end this madness.

Broderick did not tackle. He thrust his knife in between Michael's shoulder blades. The knife tore deeply into bone and viscera. Broderick struck again—and again. When he finally removed the knife, the blood poured in rivers. He reached down and searched Michael's body for weapons.

"My daughter worshipped you. You used her up and spat her out. This is your justice, Michael Black."

Meredith knelt by Michael and looked at Quinn's father. The blood pooled around them. She reached for the manuscript and put it in a dry spot. She turned back to Michael and could see his light dimming.

Broderick took the knife, held in his gloved right hand, and held it out for Meredith, who took it instinctively.

"You deserve whatever happens next," Broderick said. "This is almost as much your fault as it is his." He nodded to Michael, whose eyes softened and adopted a faraway look, letting everyone know he was never coming back.

# CHAPTER 81

Broderick turned and walked out the door. He listened closely to see if Meredith would follow, but he doubted she would.

He was proud of himself. He thought of putting the knife in her hand while he crouched in the closet in a position no man his age should. He walked briskly across the hall to the other room, stripped his bloody shirt and retrieved his tools, which were sitting on the bed.

When he left his room, he again checked to see if Meredith had followed. She hadn't. Feeling the adrenaline of a dozen racing horses, he calmly walked to the clerk's desk and handed her the second half of the two thousand dollars he promised her. He could tell by the look on her face she needed the money. He reached over and grabbed the cartridge out of the player that had been videotaping all the entrances and exits to the hotel.

"You never saw me." He nodded and made sure she nodded back.

"Who?" she asked.

When he got to the door, he looked over his shoulder at the woman. "Hell's gonna come," he warned.

"Hell's here every day." She said it in a way he needed to hear.

Thirty seconds later, Broderick headed back to Atlanta, having closed the most horrible chapter of his life.

# CHAPTER 82

Meredith crumbled like a rag doll. She sat motionless as the devil bled out onto the carpet in front of her. She still had the knife clutched tightly in her hand. She would be charged with murder again. She should get up, follow Quinn's father, and take pictures of him. But her body felt like cement. She could barely move a finger. She heard the gurgling, the low, constant moans. She closed her eyes and moved closer to him.

He looked up at her.

She couldn't save him now, and they both knew it.

"You know I'll always love you," Michael said in a whisper.

She looked at him with tears in her eyes and nodded.

Michael's breath grew even more shallow.

She could hear the blood collecting in his lungs and then his breathing stopped. She squeezed his hand and felt no response.

Her phone rested on the nightstand. She dropped the knife without trying to wipe it off. She swiped, his blood on her fingers leaving glaring red smears.

She wondered whether she should call anyone. She didn't know yet.

* * *

After she put the phone down, not having the courage yet to talk to Scott, she looked at the manuscript. Blood had splattered on her legs, and she had no doubt it covered her face, too.

Meredith grabbed the stack of papers. She couldn't avoid dealing with this death, and she didn't care about her appearance.

She flipped to the cover of the manuscript Michael had brought in. *Southern Gothic*, it read. Her heart sank. He hadn't handed her *Creeping Vines*. Michael must have switched it out and given her something different to send to the publisher.

Michael lay there, dead on the ground, and Meredith sat in a pool of his blood. For better or worse, she was finally rid of him. Her love affair with Michael Black and his books were the vivid scenes from the world's worst nightmare.

She would read one final work. His pupil till the end.

* * *

# SOUTHERN GOTHIC
## A NOVEL

## BY MEREDITH HARPER

# PART I
# HEAVEN

"To put meaning in one's life may end in madness,
But life without meaning is the torture
Of restlessness and vague desire—
It is a boat longing for the sea and yet afraid."
—Edgar Lee Masters, *Spoon River Anthology*

## CHAPTER 1

The letter came to the bookstore Wednesday morning, postmarked Savannah. The stationery was expensive and regal, and although it was not embossed with any initials, it felt important. It was addressed to Ms. Meredith Harper, Southern Gothic Bookstore in a powerful script, the angular letters formed with a fountain pen. The thick strokes of blue ink looked familiar to the recipient; she knew the handwriting but couldn't place it.

The envelope's inner lining was the same dark blue as the ink. She lifted the note card out gingerly, not wanting to smear any message:

Dear M:
I will call you today. An opportunity awaits.

Yours forever,
M

* * *

Meredith knew this story. It was hers. With tears in her eyes, she read on. She needed to know how it ended.

She remembered the syringe of heroin Michael had mentioned. It was probably in his pocket. She would read for a while, and if she didn't like what she read, she had more than one way out.

# AFTERWORD
# HISTORY AND MYSTERY

Like all great novels, *Southern Gothic* got its beginnings poolside at a Doubletree in Memphis, Tennessee. You know, *Anna Karenina*, *On the Road*, all of the good ones started by the pool at a Doubletree. It's a fact.

My agent, Italia Gandolfo, had given me something to ponder a week before I left on vacation to Georgia: *what are you writing next?*

I had just completed my novel *Sabotage* and hadn't really given it much thought. I had a couple of projects I had spent a little time with but no overarching goals. As I left Georgia, I had zero idea.

That was a Sunday, and I thought about it all week. Really thought about it. But I didn't have anything. I had a writing teacher in college, Bob Earleywine, who encouraged all his students to let such things rest in the subconscious. I did this while traveling back from Georgia to Memphis, one of my favorite American cities, with my mom and my three kids after seeing the sights at Muscle Shoals.

My 13-year-old, Mary, stayed in the hotel room, worrying about

One Direction and staring at her iDevice, as she sometimes is wont to do. The two younger kids, 11-year-old Sara and 9-year-old Matt, wanted to go swimming, so I accompanied them. At the indoor/outdoor pool, I thought again about Italia's seemingly simple question, but I asked it in a different way: *what would I like to read?*

It made all the difference. I remembered the scary, atmospheric novels I gobbled up when I first took up reading "adult" books, around the time I went into high school. *Harvest Home*, *Helter Skelter*, *In Cold Blood* and dozens more. I hadn't really ever considered writing those exact types of things before, and it seemed interesting. And then I looked outside.

On a brick wall across the way, a light hung. The first thoughts I had upon seeing it were memories of Savannah—fall nights, the squares filled with ghosts and mist . . . you know, Southern Gothic types of scenes. I thought if that were the kind of story I would write, it would also make a great title. A female protagonist came to mind, one who reminded me of my cousin Jennifer, who led me to so many of those books.

A few minutes later, I went back to the hotel room and collected Mary. The kids and I went for a late dessert, and we hashed out many thoughts. Sara, who is very into symbolism, came up with the last name "Black" for the villain. Matt filled in the first name. Mary came up with details, and we hatched about seventy percent of the plot on the spot.

The idea for the main story never really changed much. There needed to be some sort of novel within a novel. I first envisioned a story about a hippie commune, which was as lame as those words would indicate. There would be dirty floors and duplicitous hippies, and it would be dreadful. Then I realized I had a story idea I might be able to use.

At the time, I lived in southwest Missouri on a beautiful piece of land. It sat about two hundred yards from the site of the Battle of Crane Creek, a skirmish held on Valentine's Day in 1862. It was also a turn on the Trail of Tears. The first time I did any metal detecting, I found a boot buckle. The next time, the kids went with me, and we found a hockey puck-sized item called a sabot, which was the end of an artillery shell. They were super cool finds, but it got me thinking about the sadness driven across the land. I wondered about a cast of characters spanning the generations and interacting with each other. Still, Georgia seemed to be a much more appropriate setting than Missouri.

When I finally got to that point, I realized there was a very special property in which I could set the story—The Shoals. I had heard about it all my life and had visited when I was a kid and even had my picture taken with my grandmother and my sister there. My Georgia cousins told me I should buy it. Other family members had tried, but the people who took it over seemed to have no interest in relinquishing it to my family.

Luckily, my cousins Terrie and Jennifer accompanied me on a summer 2016 trip back to the place, and we were able to look at the house. I was pretty much done with the writing and was struck at how similar my imagined house was with this one. The only thing different, sadly, was the poor condition of the house itself. I sincerely hope it can still be restored.

Many of the historical details in the book are correct as far as I know them. Colonel Bird purchased the property after the Revolutionary War and built a house across the river from the house just like he does in *Southern Gothic*. He sold the land to my ancestor Thomas Cheely (my grandmother was a Cheely) around 1812. Cheely built the house around 1825. My family lived there through the Civil War and all that went on with it: sparing the house and burning the mills—all the drama and history a novelist could hope for.

Having only a few newspaper clippings and the memories of my relatives to go on (and the cute photo of my grandmother with my sister Elizabeth and me), I used the details I had and began writing. The novel within a novel changed several times, but it wasn't until the home stretch that it changed most dramatically.

My friend Heather Burns has edited my writing in some capacity since college. She read the book and really liked it, but she kindly told me *Red Ribbon* could be better. I can't say I disagreed with this assessment at all, and I searched for ways within my deadline of how I could give it more pop. I realized I had only done minimal research on the people who were actually at The Shoals during the winter of 1864, when it was an integral part of Sherman's march to the sea.

Because I generally knew where I wanted this story to wind up, I didn't think about checking the actual history. When I did, I was shocked. General Kilpatrick, who had spared The Shoals and not set it aflame, was not some kindly leader maintaining the peace, but a man who had been disgraced during his leadership and very much sent into exile during the march.

The Union promoted Kilpatrick through the ranks very quickly. He came in as a lieutenant in 1861 and accepted three more promotions that year. He was the first officer to be injured in the war, at the Battle of Big Bethel, and by the time he had earned the title of colonel in the second Battle of Bull Run, he began to make his name—although not always in good ways. He lost a full squadron of troops in an ill-advised campaign.

His manner made him enemies, but his star kept rising, and he became a general just before Gettysburg. But trouble struck in early 1864.

Kilpatrick raided near Richmond, hoping to free union prisoners of war. He tried to capture General Lee and other Confederate officials but couldn't get close to Richmond. Another Union officer, Colonel Ulric Dahlgren, tried to rally his troops for such an exercise but failed. With a slave who claimed to know the way, he returned to where he thought Kilpatrick would be. The slave told Dahlgren where to cross the river, but the river had swelled, and the troops found the travel difficult. When they returned, Dahlgren had the slave hanged, which understandably spurred riots. As they again tried to raid Richmond, Dahlgren was killed in action.

When Dahlgren's body was found, there were papers indicating he had formed a plot against Southern leadership and had called for the death of Jefferson Davis. This plot, in modern parlance, went viral. When combined with the hanging of the slave and another slave death brought on by a northern soldier not wanting to take orders from a slave, the entire affair gave Kilpatrick a bad name, and the East no longer welcomed him.

Kilpatrick joined forces with General Sherman, who was not a fan but understood the man's appeal—"I know that Kilpatrick is a hell of a damned fool, but I want just that sort of man to command my cavalry on this expedition." He was injured again in battle and missed several months of action, and then ended up at The Shoals during Sherman's March to the Sea.

Interestingly, after the war, he had plenty of adventures. He was twice dispatched as envoy to Chile, where he married.

His great granddaughters include Gloria Vanderbilt, and his great-great grandson is Anderson Cooper from CNN.

It's funny how things work out and stories climb from the crevices of our minds. I don't think I have ever had this much fun writing something, and I certainly hope you had fun reading it.

"The Intern is smart, funny, and tough . . . one of the best mysteries I've read."

—Kinky Friedman, Governor of the Heart of Texas

# The Intern

## Dale Wiley

# The Intern

A political action thriller by Dale Wiley

It's 1995, and life is great for Washington, DC intern Trent Norris. But life can change in a moment—and does when Trent becomes the prime suspect in two murders and a slew of other crimes. Overnight, he becomes the most wanted man in America.

Trent has to find a way—any way—out. He holes up at The Watergate on a senator's dime and enlists a call girl as his unwitting ally. But with the media eating Trent alive, he doesn't have long before they catch him.

From the tony clubs of Georgetown to murders on Capitol Hill, The Intern has all the twists and turns of a classic DC thriller, with an added comedic flair.

SABOTAGE

DALE WILEY

BESTSELLING AUTHOR OF THE INTERN

# Sabotage

An espionage action thriller by Dale Wiley

**Every hour, explosions rock the United States.**

Without warning of where or when they will occur. Big cities, small towns, and rural back roads. Sinister messages appear on computer screens across America, and that message is clear.

**No one is safe...**

- Not disgraced FBI agent Grant, awaiting his call back to the big time;

- Not rapper Pal Joey, an international sensation;

- Not savvy beauty Caitlin, the ultimate "Sin City" party girl;

- Not even Naseem, the would-be martyr who helped plan the attacks.

An unhinged mastermind paralyzes a nation, and unlikely heroes must put aside their differences and forge an alliance to stop the attacks before the passing hours bring down a Nation.

All roads lead to Las Vegas. Can four people, united only by their hatred of a common enemy stop ... Sabotage?

# Other Titles from Vesuvian Books

*Hell has a new master*

# BLACKWELL

By Alexandrea Weis with Lucas Astor

In the late 1800s, handsome, wealthy New Englander, Magnus Blackwell, is the envy of all.

When Magnus meets Jacob O'Conner—a Harvard student from the working class—an unlikely friendship is forged. But their close bond is soon challenged by a captivating woman; a woman Magnus wants, but Jacob gets.

Devastated, Magnus seeks solace in a trip to New Orleans. After a chance meeting with Oscar Wilde, he becomes immersed in a world of depravity and brutality, inevitably becoming the inspiration for Dorian Gray. Armed with the forbidden magic of voodoo, he sets his sights on winning back the woman Jacob stole from him.

Amid the trappings of Victorian society, two men, bent on revenge, will lay the foundation for a curse that will forever alter their destinities.

KILLING
JANE

STACY GREEN

***What if everything you've ever heard about Jack the Ripper is wrong…***

A young woman is brutally murdered in Washington D.C., and the killer leaves behind a calling card connected to some of the most infamous murders in history.

*Jack the Ripper*

Rookie homicide investigator Erin Prince instinctively knows the moment she sees the mutilated body that it's only a matter of time before someone else dies.

She and her partner, Todd Beckett, are on the trail of a madman, and a third body sends them in the direction they feared most: a serial killer is walking the streets of D.C.

*The clock is ticking.*

Erin must push past her mounting self-doubt in order to unravel a web of secrets filled with drugs, pornography, and a decades old family skeleton before the next victim is sacrificed.

*The only way to stop a killer is to beat them at their own game.*

CHILDREN OF THE FIFTH SUN

2012 WASN'T THE END
IT WAS THE BEGINNING

"A BIT TOM CLANCY, A HINT OF DAN BROWN"
-CHARITY SCRIPTURE, AMAZON

GARETH WORTHINGTON

# COMING 2.28.17

# CHILDREN OF THE FIFTH SUN

## By Gareth Worthington

**Genre:** "Science Faction" - science fiction, action and adventure with fact-based science, theories and mythology

IN ALMOST EVERY BELIEF SYSTEM ON EARTH, there exists a single unifying mythos: thousands of years ago a great flood devastated the Earth's inhabitants. From the ruins of this cataclysm, a race of beings emerged from the sea bestowing knowledge and culture upon humanity, saving us from our selfish drive toward extinction. Some say this race were "ancient aliens" who came to assist our evolution.

But what if they weren't alien at all? What if they evolved right here on Earth, alongside humans … and they are still here? *And, what if the World's governments already know?*

***

Kelly Graham is a narcissistic self-assured freelance photographer specializing in underwater assignments. While on a project in the Amazon with his best friend, Chris D'Souza, a mysterious and beautiful government official, Freya Nilsson, enters Kelly's life and turns it upside down. Her simple request to retrieve a strange object from deep underwater puts him in the middle of an international conspiracy. A conspiracy that threatens to change the course of human history.

**www.childrenofthefifthsun.com**